TOTALLY UNSUITABLE
FOR CHILDREN

Books by the same author

Jeremy Brown of the Secret Service
Jeremy Brown and the Mummy's Curse
Jeremy Brown on Mars
They Melted His Brain!

TOTALLY UNSUITABLE FOR CHILDREN

SIMON CHESHIRE

WALKER BOOKS
AND SUBSIDIARIES
LONDON • BOSTON • SYDNEY

K MOV I C
638180278
9/00

First published 2000 by Walker Books Ltd
87 Vauxhall Walk, London SE11 5HJ

2 4 6 8 10 9 7 5 3 1

Text © 2000 Simon Cheshire
Jacket illustration © 2000 Hunt Emerson

This book has been typeset in Sabon.

Printed and bound in Great Britain by
Creative Print and Design (Wales), Ebbw Vale

British Library Cataloguing in Publication Data
A catalogue record for this book is available from
the British Library.

ISBN 0-7445-5936-7

*To the real-life George,
who spoke fluent alien*

CHAPTER ONE

"Ladies and gentlemen! The final act in tonight's show is TOTALLY unsuitable for children!"

The audience went, "Ooooooo."

"What you are about to see," continued the showman, "has sent savage beasts white with fear! It has caused shock, horror, and many terrible cases of squirty tummy!"

The audience went, "Eeeeeee."

"Ladies and gentlemen! We present, the one! The only! Dennis Biggs and his Cabinet of Death!"

The showman flung his arms wide, and his eyes even wider. He was tall and wiry, with a thick moustache which stuck out at each side of his round face. His name was Julian Chimes and he was in charge of everything. The glow from the lights along the edge of the stage made the thousands of sequins sewn on to his long coat glitter in a hundred colours.

The band was squashed into the tiny orchestra pit in front of the first row of seats. They quickly flipped over to the next page of their music sheets and struck up a creepy tune. They dodged and ducked in time with the music in order to avoid each other's arms and legs as they played.

Shadows flickered around the Victorian theatre. They danced across the beautifully decorated ceiling. They skipped along the elegantly shaped balconies. They got lost in the folds of the huge, heavy red curtain, and the fringe of yellow tassels along its base.

The curtain rose to reveal a short man and a tall box. Both were dressed in black, but only the man wore a top hat. Unlike Julian, Dennis Biggs wasn't in charge of anything. He stepped forward, doing his best to look strange and mysterious.

"Can I have a fearless volunteer please?" he cried in a flat voice.

Claws and tentacles were waved in the air. In that night's audience there were no Earthlings at all. The lack of humanoids was unfortunate, because Dennis Biggs's cabinet was designed to fit someone with only two legs and one head.

"Er... Um..." said Dennis. He shielded his eyes from the glare of the stage lights, searching for a hand. Or at least, a hand with five fingers.

"I'll do it!" came a squeal from the darkness in front of him. "Me! I'll do it!"

A very large Gastropule rippled up to Dennis on her slimy belly. She waved a couple of tentacles at her friends in row C, with half her face full of eyes blinking nervously. A little giggle escaped from her favourite mouth.

Dennis glanced at Julian, who was now standing offstage in the wings. Julian paddled his hand at him, as if to say, "The show must go on, so get on with it."

"Give this brave young lady a big round of applause, ladies and gentlemen," cried Dennis. The audience hooted and cheered.

"Now then," said Dennis. "What is your name?"

"My name's Glubbla," said the Gastropule, giggling.

"Smashing. And where are you from, Glubbla?"

"I'm from the third moon of Zephlon Beta."

Her friends in row C whistled loudly. A couple of them flung showers of popcorn through the air. Dennis raised a hand for silence. The serious expression on his face hushed the audience, and they waited expectantly. A group of Andromedan Sand Lizards were so frozen with anticipation that they accidentally dribbled venom on to their ice-creams. The ice-creams turned red.

"And now!" cried Dennis. "Prepare your

minds for boggling, my friends. Shield your nerves from fear. For now, I will slice Glubbla into eight pieces ... in my Cabinet of Death!"

The audience went, "Aaaaaaaaa." Glubbla went slightly wobbly.

Dennis flung open the front of the cabinet to reveal a blood-red interior. Black slots marked the eight slicing points.

"Glubbla, you will now please ... step into the cabinet!"

Glubbla giggled. With a last glance at her friends she shuffled past Dennis. She managed to wedge most of her tentacles, about half her head and a bit of her T-shirt into the box. Then she got stuck.

She squealed and twittered, not sure whether to push or pull. The audience peered closer, not sure whether this was part of the act or not. Dennis took a running jump at her from behind and forced another couple of tentacles in. Glubbla squeaked in alarm. Her eyelids all started fluttering at once.

Grumbles began to emerge from here and there in the audience. They were starting to realize that Glubbla really shouldn't be turning mauve like that. Dennis gave her bottom a couple of hefty kicks, but that only made her twitter all the more.

The grumbles rapidly merged into a pool of discontent. Dennis loosened the collar of his shirt. He grabbed two armfuls of Glubbla and heaved up, left, right, up again.

Squiirrrt-PHHPHHHH-PLATT!

The huge sac of digestive juices on Glubbla's back burst like a wet balloon. Dennis, the cabinet and the band were drenched in stinging acidic slime.

"I was saving that to dunk my dinner in!" squealed Glubbla tearfully.

The audience went, "Booooooo!"

"Look at it!" cried Dennis. "Look at my Cabinet of Death! You've ruined the paintwork!"

The audience also went, "Gerroff!", "Rubbish!" and "We want our credits back!" Dennis, still dripping, stormed off stage just as Julian came rushing on.

"Ladies and gentlemen," called Julian, flashing his best smile. "Merely a slight technical hitch. The management would like to assure you that—"

The audience yelled, "Shaddup! We're going home!" Glubbla's friends carried the cabinet away with Glubbla still in it. Her bottom slapped back and forth as they hurried for the exit.

Backstage, a boy called George sat at the long bank of controls which operated the theatre's lights, scenery and food dispensers. He had an angelic face and a mop of fair hair, and he wore battered old zero-grav overalls. Like Julian and Dennis he was a human, but unlike

11

Julian and Dennis he would hardly have made it into his teens if his age had been counted in Earth years. He swivelled around in his chair, munching on a fish and lemon curd sandwich.

"Well, that went down like a cup of cold sick, didn't it Dennis?" he said cheerfully. Bits of bread sprayed on to the floor as he spoke.

"Tourists!" spat Dennis. "I keep saying we shouldn't do these in-flight shows."

They could hear a distant ka-bleep ka-bleep coming from the front of the theatre. Mrs Tikkitz, the robot box office, was stamping the audience's credit cards with full refunds as they left.

On stage, the curtain fell. The band started to pack up for the night. Julian joined George and Dennis. He closed his eyes and put a weary hand to his forehead.

"Ruination," he sighed. "We face a bleak future full of poverty and hunger, my dear colleagues, if we keep on having to cough up the readies like that."

"Riffraff," mumbled Dennis. "And they've nicked my cabinet. Dregs of the universe, the lot of them."

"They, Biggs," cried Julian, "are our public. When I was but a humble floor-scrubber at the Black Hole Concert Hall, they used to say to me, 'Julian, the customer is always right.' And they were perfectly correct. If the audience thinks you're rubbish and wants its dosh back,

12

Biggs, then so be it. It's all part of the magic of the theatre."

"Blow the magic of the theatre," said the sharp voice of the Great Projecto. "He's cost us a night's wages!"

The show's performers were gathered from many points in time and space: Projecto was a hairless, three-eyed being from the planet Volpok. His stage act involved firing his own ear wax at various novelty targets, by building up pressure beneath his brain. Thanks to this regular clearing-out, his hearing was absolutely brilliant. He had heard the conversation from over in the performers' dressing-room, and had come out to interrupt it.

"I demand that Biggs be removed from the show!" he cried. His blue skin turned green with fury.

Dennis prided himself on his ability to come up with witty one-liners in situations like this. In this particular situation, he came up with: "Bog off, bumhead!"

Julian patted their backs gently. "Now now, gentlemen, there's no need for us to behave in such a manner. Let us not forget that we are professional artistes. We rise above such petty problems. We concern ourselves with more worthy things."

The Great Projecto gave Dennis a smack in the mouth. They grappled. Projecto dragged Dennis towards the dressing-room.

"You can come and explain to the rest of the performers why we can't afford to get the costumes cleaned again this week!" he grunted.

George stuffed down the last of his sandwich. He swivelled in his chair, and his shadow did a somersault on the stripy wallpaper. He looked out of the tall sash window beside him. Stars drifted past, but he didn't recognize any of the constellations. The dozens of vehicles owned by tonight's audience were vanishing into the distance. They scattered in all directions, leaving thin trails of ion vapour glowing faintly against the blackness of space.

Julian sighed. "George, my boy, this has not been the most successful of evenings."

"Mmmm," agreed George. "I think we might be in need of one or two new acts to liven up the show."

"Quite right, George, as always," grinned Julian, holding up a finger. "And by the best of good fortune, only this afternoon I received news of a possible addition to our cast. I have already arranged for us to make an extra stop along the way to our next scheduled landing."

George's eyes narrowed. "Extra stop where?" he said at last.

"Oh, um, just a refuelling station. Nowhere special, nowhere terribly interesting."

"What 'possible addition'?"

"Something, I am reliably informed, both spectacular and unusual. A marvel of the natural world, so I'm led to believe. Now run along, my boy, I'm sure you have jobs to do, props to fix, that sort of thing."

Julian, whistling merrily to himself, hurried away before George could ask any more questions. George watched him go. Suspicious thoughts tiptoed nervously through his mind. He wiped a dribble of mayonnaise off his chin.

The theatre flew on through space, with the powerful engines in its basement humming steadily and the solar panels on its roof soaking up power from the light of the stars. Both its outside and inside appeared to be Victorian because that style of decor had been very fashionable last time it went in for a refit. Its tough outer shell had been specially moulded to look like real bricks and mortar. Its next scheduled landing was on the planet where the Victorian style had originated – a watery, ice-capped planet in Sector J, dotted with deserts, cities and grassy patches.

Meanwhile, on this same watery planet in Sector J, Sophie Ottershaw was finishing her homework. Her fingers flew across the keyboard of her PC, rapidly tapping out a detailed explanation of how Napoleon's defeat at Waterloo in 1815 was a direct result of his war with Russia. She ended her essay, e-mailed it to her history teacher, and ticked off item 12 on her "To Do" list, which was: "Complete

15

work by 8:45p.m."

The clock above her bed said 8:37p.m. She smiled to herself and nodded happily at nobody in particular. She always felt better when things were back on schedule.

"Ottershaw Averts Homework Deadline Crisis," she said. Her words landed softly in the cushions scattered tastefully around her peaceful, smartly decorated room. The computer sat exactly square on her desk. Her sharpened pencils stood to attention in her "Souvenir of Weymouth" mug. She always felt better when things were tidy. The many dozens of books on her shelves were arranged according to size and colour. Her hair and clothes were equally neat.

An open packet of chewy Squeezi-Mints sat on her bedside cabinet. She popped one into her mouth, dropped its wrapping into the wastepaper basket, and made a selection of "mmmm" noises.

However, she was just playing for time. Now that she'd caught up on her history essay, she knew that she couldn't avoid going down-stairs any longer. The book she was currently reading (*Expand Your Career in Journalism*), had been left under the coffee table in the living-room. She'd never be able to sleep without at least an hour's study of Chapter 2 ("First Steps to Success"), so downstairs she would have to go.

"Ottershaw In Book Fetching Shock," she mumbled.

She sighed and left the room, pausing only to make sure the light was switched off. She heard her father at his piano before she reached the foot of the stairs.

ping ... ping ping ping ping ping...

"La la laaaa," he sang, on the same note as the pings.

The door to his study was wide open. Sophie would have to pass it on her way to the living-room. Maybe ... if she stepped ... very quietly ... along the—

"Who's that?" His booming voice made her jump. His wild black hair and even wilder, blacker beard would have made anyone jump, but Sophie was used to them. He tugged at the edges of his tatty old cardigan.

"It's me, Dad. I've been upstairs doing my history essay, remember?"

"Oh. Yes," mumbled Dad, remembering. "You've been up there for four hours. I don't know where you get these obsessive habits."

ping ... ping ping ping...

A dozen sheets of music paper were perched on a stand next to the piano. He ripped them into tiny pieces and dropped them into the overflowing wastepaper basket by his feet. "No. No no no no no!" he huffed. "Should be C major. Sophie, must you stand there? It's very distracting. I'm trying to work."

17

Sophie started edging towards the living-room. Dad suddenly turned towards her.

"And I forbid you to go to that party!" he cried.

"What party?" said Sophie.

"That one, you know," grumbled Dad, waving a hand at her. His bushy black eyebrows knotted themselves together into a frown. "Near the shops. Big ugly red house."

"Dad, that was two years ago."

"Oh... Did you go?"

"No."

"Good. Now run along, please, there's a good girl!"

Sophie took a deep breath. "You won't forget I'm going to be late home tomorrow, will you? I'm interviewing the mayor for the school newspaper."

"For the what?"

"Dad, I'm the editor."

Dad muttered something to himself. Sophie was about to run along, please, there's a good girl, when she remembered to ask: "Is Mum in yet?"

"No. I don't think so. Important meeting or something."

ping ... ping ping...

Sophie went on her way, paying no attention at all to the poster of Dad's most recent triumph. The poster was framed and hung up in the hallway, announcing "The First Perfor-

18

mance of Vladimir Ottershaw's New Masterpiece, Piano Concerto No. 96". She fetched her book, retreated to her room, and eventually drifted off to sleep with Chapter 2 still open on the bedcovers in front of her.

The Ottershaws' house stood alone on the far edge of the town, surrounded on all sides by fields. Sophie was a light sleeper, and so she couldn't help but notice when a whopping great theatre landed in the field next to the house, belching bright green smoke from its engines.

It was in the early hours of the following morning. A crescent moon glowed sleepily, and the sky couldn't quite decide whether to be a simple black or a stylish navy blue. The theatre floated to the ground, crushing six crisp packets, two empty drinks cans and a very startled mole.

Sophie's face was pressed against the window of her room. Her eyes went all boggly, in a way which would have made any optician seriously worried. What in the name of the national papers was THAT? And what did that sign at the front say? "The Galactic Coliseum"?

Inside the theatre, George was asking similar questions, but about something rather different. He and Julian were in one of the storerooms tucked away in the basement. In front of them was a metal cage.

"What in the name of the Saturn Nebula is THAT?" cried George.

"That, George, my lad," said Julian proudly, "is our new feature attraction. And what a splendidly handsome beast he is too!"

"What's he called?" said George nervously.

"He is of the species Repticus Incisorops. Native of ... some planet or other, so I am reliably informed. It's all there on the label."

George reached for the slip of card tied to the cage with a ragged length of string. The creature hissed and snapped at his hand. He snatched it back quickly.

"Where did you get him, Julian?" he said seriously, getting a weird sinking feeling that was nothing to do with the theatre's landing. "Who did you get him from?"

"Mere details, boy, mere details. Don't worry about little things like that, think of the crowds he will attract. Think how our public will clamour for just a brief glimpse of him! Fame and fortune stand waiting in the wings, you mark my words. It'll be just like the old days, when I did my cutlery juggling routine at the Apollo on Speltron IV. How they gasped! How they screamed for more! Come along, George, we must let our new friend rest, we have much to prepare."

The creature coiled itself around the bars of the cage. It was roughly as big as a medium-sized dog, with two powerful hind legs and crab-like pincers at the ends of its three arms. Its head was bony and covered with scales. Two silvery eyes, with pupils like a cat's, scanned every inch of its new home. A thin tongue glistened its way along short, jagged teeth.

George didn't like the look of it one little bit. In the days to come, he'd wish he'd been able to prevent its arrival on Earth.

CHAPTER TWO

Bright sunshine quickly dried up the morning dew on the grass, as if it was embarrassed to have all that moisture lying around on a hot June day like this. It was barely breakfast time, but already the temperature was rising rapidly.

Sophie hadn't given the weather a moment's thought. She was still at her bedroom window, spending half the time staring out at the theatre and the other half scribbling furiously in her wire-bound, reporter-style notebook. As editor of the school newspaper, it was her duty to record every detail of this ... whatever it was.

"Ottershaw Scoops Major News Event," she mumbled to herself. She made a quick note at the top of today's "To Do" list to get a new battery for her camera. "Full Story, With Pics!"

She popped her notebook into her pocket,

straightened up her school uniform (flicking a bit of fluff off the shoulder), and checked she'd put her clean hockey kit in her bag. After a last glance out of the window, she went downstairs. This morning's schedule: breakfast; a quick preliminary investigation of the ... whatever it was; bus; double maths.

Mum was in the kitchen, sacking one of her employees on her mobile phone. She stabbed the phone's Off button and went back to nibbling a piece of dry toast.

"Sophie," nodded Mum.

"Mum," nodded Sophie.

The fridge was almost empty. Sophie pursed her lips, sighed, and added "Shopping" to her "To Do" list.

"Mum, there's no fruit juice. And there are no eggs. And there's no bacon. How can I have a proper breakfast without vitamins and protein and stuff?"

"Can't you make something from what there is?" mumbled Mum. She was leafing through a file labelled "Sales Pattern Analysis", and didn't look up.

"What, from a little dollop of butter and half a sausage? Even a TV chef couldn't make anything out of that! I'll simply have to forget about eating." Sophie stared at Mum crossly. Mum still didn't look up. "I'll just die of hunger on the way to the bus stop, then."

"Mmm, yes darling," mumbled Mum.

23

"Lovely." Suddenly she snapped the file shut and jumped to her feet. She flicked her wrist up towards her face. Her watch displayed the current time, the time in New York, and a countdown to her first meeting of the day. "Must dash. Needed at the office. How do I look?"

Sophie eyed Mum's severe red suit, pointed pale face and neatly rounded black hairdo. "Like you'd sell Granny to a sausage factory," she said sadly.

"Excellent," said Mum. "First rule of business: image is everything."

She headed for the hall. Sophie trotted along behind her.

"Have you seen that ... whatever it is out in the field?" said Sophie. "I'm going to go and investigate it for the school newspaper."

"Err, yes, I did catch sight of something through the bathroom window. Marvellous what they achieve with National Lottery cash."

By the time Sophie had finished saying, "It didn't come from the Lottery, it came from the sky," Mum had already slammed the front door behind her.

Sophie stood alone in the hall listening to the *ping ... ping ping ping* coming from the study.

At the same moment, over at the theatre, George stood alone in the corridor outside the basement storeroom listening to the GGrrrr-AKKKhh AkHHGG coming from the cage inside. The creature was restless. George was restless too, but for different reasons. He didn't like the idea of any wild animal being locked up. On the other hand, the idea of this particular wild animal roaming free struck him as even worse.

He wandered through the auditorium. Dennis and the Great Projecto were both on stage trying to practise their acts at the same time. So they mostly just poked each other in the eye. Other performers were gossiping with the band or sipping coffee in the front row. Among them were a horned, goggle-eyed Plutonian (Zok, Interstellar Stand-up Comic) and the two-headed Scanna Reedowt (Singer of Sad Songs in Stereo). High above George's head, a gang of furry creatures were busying themselves around the stage lights. They were part spider, part guinea pig, and so were ideally suited to light electrical work. George, being Stage Manager, was their boss.

"Hey girls, don't forget to put the blue filters in for the opening dance routine!" he called. They chirped tunefully in reply.

George made his way outside, cupping his hands over his eyes to block the glare of the sunshine. He looked around, at the fields, at that house over there, at the young female human walking towards the theatre. So this was it, eh? This was the planet he'd been born on. This was Earth.

"Bit of a dump, really," he said to himself.

Julian was pasting up huge billboard posters around the theatre's gleaming main entrance. He overheard George and tut-tutted loudly.

"Dump, boy? Dump? Earth is not a dump, it is an opportunity twice over. For one, we have the opportunity to meet fellow humans, which is a rare treat for us, as you know. For two, we have the opportunity to bring our own brand of showbiz glamour to this beautiful but far-off sector of the galaxy."

"And for three, you've got the opportunity to fleece the locals of a few credits."

Julian sighed wearily. "Such vulgar considerations are furthest from my thoughts, lad. But a flipping great mound of cash would come in jolly useful, you're right. Hence these new posters!"

At that moment there was a hem-hem-I'm-here cough behind them. They turned to find Sophie, notebook at the ready. She marched up to Julian, hand thrust out.

"Sophie Ottershaw, Editor, local school newspaper," she announced. "Pleased to meet you."

"The press!" cried Julian, shaking Sophie's hand much too vigorously for her liking. "Delighted, young lady, delighted! It's always a pleasure to make contact with representa-

26

tives of the media, with those who can carry news of our arrival far and wide."

"Thank you," said Sophie politely. "I'd like to ask you a couple of questions, if that'd be all right?"

"By all means, dear girl. Fire away."

"OK," said Sophie. She smiled up at Julian, with her pencil poised over her notebook. "What IS this thing, who ARE you people, and WHY are you here?"

"Oh. How refreshingly direct. This, my dear, is the Galactic Coliseum theatre, and I, Julian Chimes, have the enormous honour and privilege of being its proprietor. Allow me to present my stage manager, George."

"Hiya," said George. He thought Sophie looked completely stuck-up.

"Hallo," said Sophie. She thought George looked like a right scruffbag. She went on: "But this ... *theatre* dropped out of the sky last night."

"We are but simple strolling players," said Julian.

"You can't take an entire theatre for a stroll," said Sophie.

"It's got engines," said George, as if Sophie had said something really daft.

"My fellow artistes are inside, resting for tonight's performance," continued Julian. "An extravaganza of music, mirth and mystery, a spectacle of such wonderment as has never been seen in this solar system! Judge for yourself." He pointed to the poster, which read:

THE GALACTIC COLISEUM

— presents —

AN EVENING

— of —

EXCEPTIONAL ENTERTAINMENT

Peerless professional performers gathered from the nineteen corners of the cosmos

☞ **PLUS** ☜
For the first time anywhere!

A FINALE FILLED WITH FRIGHT!

A creature so strange, so terrible, we DARE NOT tell you more!

FOR A LIMITED PERIOD ONLY
8p.m. LOCAL TIME, EVERY NIGHT
Unevolved species half price

"You're all *aliens*?" said Sophie. She looked them up and down for a moment. "You two don't look like aliens."

"Absolutely right, young lady. I am an Earthling," said Julian. "And so, by happy coincidence, is George. However, this is the very first time he's visited the planet since he was a few days old. I wonder, Miss Ottershaw, if you would be so kind as to take him under your wing—"

"Julian!" cried George.

"—show him the sights. Tell him a little about his planet of origin. Perhaps you could invite him to tea, if that is still the custom in this sector?"

"JULIAN!" cried George. He needn't have protested, because Sophie found the suggestion totally revolting.

On the other hand, she thought, if I'm going to be a serious journalist I must learn to be fair and impartial. I must conduct proper investigations. Even if he is a right scruffbag.

"OK," she said. She turned to George. "Five o'clock at my house, over there."

"Splendid!" said Julian. "And of course I'll have two free, complimentary, no-credits-required tickets waiting for you tonight at the box office. Think of them as a reward for all the wonderful work you'll do telling your readers how brilliant the show is and how quickly they must rush to see it. See you later!"

"Thanks," said Sophie, not sure she was thankful at all. She headed for the bus stop.

At something getting on for six o'clock that evening, George headed for the house. He'd only seen Earth buildings on the Teach-'n'-

Learn screen he'd had when he was younger, and he was surprised at how small a real one looked close up.

"You're late," said Sophie, opening the front door as he approached. She couldn't tell whether the expression on his face meant he didn't understand, or he didn't care. Either way, it annoyed her even more. She hurried him through to the kitchen.

She took a deep breath and put on the voice she used when making announcements about the school newspaper in assembly. "This is a typical room where Earth people prepare food."

"Oh wooooow," said George sarcastically. "And there was me thinking kitchens were for hanging your clothes in."

"I'm only trying to be helpful," said Sophie.

"Food would be helpful. Is that your cold storage unit?"

"That's our 'fridge', yes."

Sophie had done the shopping after school, so the fridge was full again. George grabbed a block of cheese and bit a big chunk out of it.

"Hey, cheese. I like cheese," he said with a grin, spraying little lumps of it over the lettuce.

Sophie grabbed it back. "That's disgusting," she cried.

"No, it's really nice. Got any jam to put on it?"

"That's also disgusting. Isn't there anything else you'd like?"

30

"Fried potato in custard?" he said. Sophie went slightly pale. "Jellied porridge?" Sophie went slightly paler.

"What's wrong with jellied porridge?" said George.

"You have a lot to learn about Earth food," said Sophie weakly.

"That IS Earth food," insisted George. "The dispensers backstage do stuff from any planet you like – cheese, jam, potato, custard, jelly, porridge, it's all on the Earth menu."

"Perhaps you'd like a nice, simple soft drink instead?" said Sophie patiently.

George thought for a moment. "Surely all drinks are soft? Otherwise they'd be solids."

"Or tea?"

"Ah, yeh, tea. I drink tea. Plenty of ketchup, please."

Suddenly Dad's voice wailed from the study. "Sophie dear! Be a good girl and stop talking, will you? Your voice is at the same pitch as this piece I'm trying to compose and it's very off-putting!"

George stood still and raised his eyebrows, as if he'd just been warned not to step in something nasty. Sophie sighed and checked through the money that was left over from the shopping.

"That's my dad," she whispered.

"Couldn't you get another one?" whispered George.

"Come on. We'll go to the Fragrant Harbour."

"Er, swimming pool?"

"Chinese takeaway."

"Oooooo... Mmmmmm... Sllluuurrrpppp!"

Dribbles of sweet and sour sauce plipped down George's overalls. He tipped back the foil tray and gulped down the last of his mushroom fried rice.

"Mushrooms and rice," he said, with his mouth still full. "It's weird, but it's tasty!" He belched.

Sophie glanced around nervously to make sure that nobody she knew was in sight. She finished off her chow mein and placed her disposable chopsticks on the paper napkin which was draped neatly across her knees.

They were sitting on the low wall which bordered the wide grassy area outside the shops. Traffic weaved in and out of the car park beyond the trees. Sophie took out her notebook.

"So," she said, in interview mode, "how did you end up in that theatre?"

"Wormhole," said George, picking at his teeth.

"I beg your pardon?"

"There's a small time-space wormhole that opens up now and again in the costume store. I dropped through it when I was a baby."

"But where did you drop through from?"

"1921, apparently. I fell out of my cot in the middle of the night, and dropped 36 trillion miles into a basket full of cowboy outfits."

"Couldn't they send you back?"

"No, it's a one-way wormhole. Most of them are. It's pretty useful though. We get a lot of pens and socks coming through. Which is good for Percy."

"Percy?"

"Percy Pottersby, Pen and Sock Swallower. Marvellous act. He downs a box of biros and a dozen woolly winter feet-warmers in a minute and a half."

"Fancy that," said Sophie, not impressed in the slightest.

"Of course, that's his stage name. Whoever heard of anyone called Percy Pottersby?"

"What's his real name?"

"Peregrine Pottersby. Interesting guy. He used to cut airholes in wellies for the Extremely Useless Rubber Boot Company." George crumpled up his foil tray and tossed it over his shoulder. Drips of grease spiralled across the grass. Without a word, Sophie picked it up between thumb and forefinger and deposited it in a nearby bin.

"And what about your Mr Chimes?" she continued.

George leaned closer to her. "Well, I don't know for sure, but the rumour in the dressing-room is that he was abducted by aliens many years ago. They beamed him aboard a mothership while he was clipping his toenails one evening." His voice suddenly dropped to a whisper. "Shhhh, say nothing. He doesn't like to talk about it."

"But he can't hear us," said Sophie.

"He might. He's over there." George pointed over Sophie's shoulder.

They could see Julian, on the other side of the road, marching purposefully from zebra crossing to tree, tree to shop, shop to car. Each time he stopped, he unrolled a poster from the bundle under his arm and glued it to something. Posters were dotted at regular intervals back along the route he'd taken. Their positions made a wiggly S shape that vanished into the distance, towards the town centre.

"I think the local council will have something to say about that," said Sophie crossly. "They like to keep the streets clean and free from litter."

"I expect that's a big relief to you, then," said George.

"There's nothing wrong with keeping things tidy," sighed Sophie.

They watched Julian run over to an old lady who was carrying two heavy bags of shopping. They saw his arms circling with enthusiasm as he spoke. She tried to walk around him. He kept in step with her, his arms swirling like the

sails of a windmill in a gale. She struggled to
pass him. He brandished two free tickets. She
whacked him on the head with a shopping
bag. He was knocked off his feet, and landed
in a flat star-shape on the road. A lorry
swerved to avoid him, hooting angrily. He
bounded back on to the pavement and continued on his way.

"Better get back," said George. "Got to
check the sound system before curtain-up.
Hey, I'll take you backstage to see our new star
attraction."

And so they returned to the theatre, where
George did indeed show Sophie the creature in
the cage. Sophie was terrified.

"If that's your star attraction, I'd hate to
meet whatever failed the audition," she shuddered. "Ottershaw In Vicious Monster
Menace," she added under her breath.

The creature growled and snapped. The
sharp pincers at the ends of its three arms
gripped the bars of its cage and shook the
whole thing violently. It stooped over as it did
so, because the cage was now on the small side.
The creature had grown to roughly the size of
a polar bear.

Sophie tried to move further away, but
found that her back was already pressed
against the wall. She clutched a half-empty
pack of Squeezi-Mints to her chest, absent-
mindedly tearing at the silver foil. The creature

made a sudden lunge for her, and she darted to one side, letting out a piercing "Aaaaahh-hhh!"

"We're going to have to find somewhere bigger for him to live," said George.

Sophie shut her eyes for a moment. Maybe it was a nightmare. Maybe she was safely tucked up in her own bed, in her own home. Maybe... Nope, still there. One of the creature's pincers flashed out towards her, snapping with a sharp KLAK-KLAK. She managed to hold in the scream this time.

"That's interesting," said George. "Something about you has him spooked."

"You don't say?" quivered Sophie. "Does ... does it have a name?"

"We had a vote on it today. Julian came up with a shortlist of suggestions. All the performers and backstage crew had to put a tick against the name they liked best, and the one with the most ticks won. Sophie, meet Twinkle."

"Twinkle?"

"Yeh. I voted for 'Derek' myself, but there you have it. I just wish Julian would tell me where he got him from."

Twinkle made another grab for Sophie. He hissed like a pit of vipers that were really cheesed off with each other's company. His pointed tongue licked at the bars.

"Perhaps we should go," said Sophie

36

quickly. "I'm meeting my form tutor Mrs Womsey before the show. She's using the other free ticket Mr Chimes gave me. Come on, *come on.*"

They left Twinkle to get on with a bit more hissing and cage-rattling. Sophie dabbed her eyes and forehead with a handkerchief as they made their way up to the auditorium.

"This place is a madhouse," she whispered to herself.

"This place is a marvel!" cried Mrs Womsey. She gave her glasses a quick wipe with the sleeve of her jumper, and went back to admiring the decoration on the ceiling of the auditorium. Her wispy hair kept wisping into the face of the man behind her, who kept making loud remarks she never noticed. "Sophie, are you going to write an article about this place for the school newspaper?"

Sophie, sitting next to her in the front row, checked her watch. The performance was late getting started. "I'm not sure. I can't think of anything positive to say yet."

"Oh no! Really?" said Mrs Womsey, putting a concerned hand to her cheek. "But surely it's wonderful what National Lottery funds can achieve."

Before Sophie could protest, the band began playing a rousing march and the house lights dimmed. The audience stopped scrunching their crisp packets and paid attention. The theatre was packed. Julian would have said this was because of his brilliant poster campaign. Anyone who knew the truth would have said it was because of the hundreds of free tickets he'd been giving out all day.

With a triumphant roll of drums from the band, the curtain rose. A dazzling white spotlight fell on Julian and his glittery coat. Makeup concealed the black eye he'd received when the old lady's shopping bag hit him.

"Ladies and gentlemen! Welcome to the greatest show on Earth! Prepare to be amazed! Prepare to be astounded! Prepare to be so impressed you'll want to come back tomorrow and pay full price! For this, ladies and gentlemen, is like nothing you've ever seen before!"

And so it was. The audience applauded wildly for the Great Projecto. They called for more of Scanna Reedowt's heart-rending ballads. They gave a standing ovation to Douglas the android and his brilliant robot-folding act. (Douglas would ask for volunteers from the audience and then, using only the electronic odds and ends from his old cardboard box, create perfect robotic copies of them to take home. Batteries not included.) Dennis Biggs didn't appear that night. He was working on a spectacular new trick, to be billed as Dennis Biggs and his Bucket of Doom.

However, the longest applause – and the

loudest gasps – were reserved for Twinkle.

"Ladies and gentlemen," cried Julian. "Our final act tonight is definitely NOT suitable for persons of a nervous disposition..."

Twinkle rose up through a trapdoor in the stage, chained by one leg to a massive steel block (into which his cage would convert at the press of a button). He kept making flying leaps for Sophie, who was furiously chewing at her Squeezi-Mints. At every leap his chain snapped tight with a CLANG and another half a dozen spectators needed a change of underwear.

"What terrific special effects," said Mrs Womsey, wriggling uncomfortably in her seat. "I expect it's a man in a rubber suit."

The audience were on their feet and cheering as Twinkle disappeared from sight, to be carried back to the storeroom on a self-steering trolley. The entire cast came back on stage for a final bow. Then back again for three curtain calls. Then back again for one more. At last the house lights came up and the audience chattered excitedly.

"Perhaps we could do a special project on the theatre this term," said Mrs Womsey enthusiastically on the way out.

"No, let's not," said Sophie.

CHAPTER THREE

It was the following day, shortly before two o'clock in the afternoon, when Twinkle attacked Sophie's school. After the previous night's show, the creature had been even more restless than usual. George was sent out to the local supermarket to buy meat. He returned from Super Save dragging a plastic sack of assorted tins, pies and frozen joints. Twinkle ate the lot, not bothering with minor details such as defrosting or using a tin-opener. Then he ate the plastic sack.

In the morning he was still restless. George hoped he was wrong, but reckoned that ever since last night Twinkle had been catching the scent of something even more delicious than a Super Save economy pork sausage. Unfortunately, he was absolutely right.

At 1:30p.m., as Twinkle was snapping the bars of his cage, Sophie was starting double

English with the rest of her class. She placed her pen, ruler and textbook in a line, level with the edge of her desk.

Meanwhile, Mrs Womsey scrawled helpful notes on the blackboard in handwriting which nobody could read. Every time she turned to speak to the class, her hair brushed up another puff of chalk dust from the board. A word which looked like "ColptxXiy" was rubbed out as she turned to announce: "Twentieth-century literature. We'll be in small groups, studying themed modules on different writers, books and styles—"

A weary groan came from somewhere at the back. Sophie glared at Wayne Banks. Mrs Womsey ignored him.

"If any of you have any ideas for projects linked to the topics we'll be discussing, then feel free to express them."

A quiet "zzzzzz" sound came from somewhere at the back again. Sophie followed Mrs Womsey's example and ignored Wayne Banks completely.

Worksheets were handed out. Sophie took a Squeezi-Mint from her pocket and chewed thoughtfully as she ran a finger down the Recommended Reading list. She nearly pointed out a spelling error to Mrs Womsey, but decided not to. She was worried it might make her look like a creep.

"What's *Animal Farm*?" moaned Wayne

Banks. "Sounds like a babies' book."

Mrs Womsey continued to ignore him. Sophie nearly pointed out that it was a classic of English literature. She also nearly pointed out that Wayne Banks ought to bloomin' well learn that there were wonderful things to be discovered if only he'd bloomin' well stop saying he was bored. But she decided not to. She was worried it might make her look like a right smarty-pants. It was while she was making these decisions that Twinkle was kicking the school gates off their hinges.

"Sounds dead boring," said Wayne Banks.

Sophie could stand it no longer. "And that just about sums you up, doesn't it, Wayne Banks," she growled. "Read the books on that list and you might, maybe, possibly, perhaps begin to start to learn something. If we're lucky."

"I think I'd rather be got by a vicious great mega-clawed, razor-toothed monster from outer space," yawned Wayne Banks. "Something like you, only which whines less."

The rest of the class erupted with laughter. Sophie fumed quietly to herself, trying to think of something clever to say. Mrs Womsey shuffled through the papers on her desk, looking for the headmaster's recent memo about dealing with classroom discipline.

They were all interrupted by the deafening smash of the windows. The pupils screamed almost as loudly as Mrs Womsey. They rushed for the door.

The rumbling screech that came from outside instantly told Sophie that it was Twinkle. The fact that the classroom was on the first floor of the building told her that Twinkle had grown again.

A huge pincer knocked out a section of wall. Gripping the sides of the hole he had made, Twinkle sprang up through the remains of the window. He was now the size of a large caravan – with an add-on tent bit at the side. As he landed, his muscular legs turned a couple of desks into splinters. His three arms spread wide, pincers snapping. His silver cat's eyes darted around the room.

Pupils crushed together in the doorway, yelling in terror. Sophie was pulled along with them. She glanced back. The creature was moving slowly towards them, sniffing, licking his lips.

Meanwhile, the headmaster was leading a group of parents along the corridor outside the classroom. He pointed out the spotlessly clean floor. He indicated the artwork done by 7C, which was pinned to a noticeboard beside a row of lockers.

"We'll now make a brief visit to a class in progress," he said, with a reassuring smile. "This is one run by our Head of English, Mrs

Womsey. Very experienced teacher. Very capable."

A tumble of pupils suddenly burst out of the classroom, screaming. Some scrambled to their feet and ran. Some, out of breath from the crush, rolled across the spotlessly clean floor. A deafening roar followed them, quickening their panic. Mrs Womsey, with her hair like an electrocuted guinea pig, emerged clutching a wad of papers to her chest. One of the lenses in her glasses had fallen out.

"Headmaster," said a parent quietly but sternly. "I thought you said you'd issued a memo about classroom discipline."

Twinkle kicked through the classroom wall. Bricks bounced off the ceiling. With a hiss like escaping steam, he leapt through a dense cloud of dust and plaster. His teeth clashed together millimetres from the headmaster's face. The headmaster fainted.

Sophie struggled to pull free from the crowd of pupils. A net of arms and faces surrounded her. The cries and screams and roars almost blotted out her thoughts. After last night, she knew it was HER that Twinkle was after. She had to get out, draw the creature away from the others.

Everyone scattered, heading for the stairs as best they could. Twinkle snatched up a parent with one pincer, and Wayne Banks with another. The parent was flung on to the top of

44

the lockers. Twinkle's snout knocked the lighting strip that ran along the ceiling. The lights swung violently to and fro, and the corridor became a shifting patchwork of brightness and shadow.

The screams of the pupils rose to a note which would have shattered glass, if there'd been any left unshattered. Sophie crawled on all fours, keeping one wall at her shoulder so she wouldn't get lost in the confusion. Wait a minute, was she heading for the stairs or back to the classroom? Her crawling motion kept scrunching up the notebook in her pocket. She wrote a report for the school newspaper in her head, to help herself think clearly.

Twinkle's thin tongue licked at Wayne Banks's face. His legs kicked wildly.

"I'll read the books! I'll read the books!" he sobbed. Twinkle snorted a high-pressure mixture of vaporized snot across Wayne Banks, then flicked him away. He was sent spinning into a group of parents.

Today, thought Sophie, *a giant monster from the far reaches of space chewed its way through the Arts Block...* She crawled faster. The claws on Twinkle's feet gouged lumps out of the floor as the monster searched in the weirdly shifting light. He kept his head low, sniffing. A hideous rattling sound gurgled at the back of his throat.

...Chewed its way through the Arts Block

and ... and ATE ME! Oh no! Oh no! So much for thinking clearly.

Several pupils had managed to find the stairs, but most of them simply kept running to wherever Twinkle wasn't. Sophie's head and sides were bashed by the knees of fleeing people. She tried to keep calm. Got to get out. Got to draw Twinkle away from the others.

"HhaaaHHSSSSSSsssss."

Every muscle in her body twitched with fright. Twinkle's face was right beside hers. Faint glimmers of light shone on the saliva that coated his teeth. His mouth opened slowly. Something smacked against her collar.

She screamed. Something pulled her backwards sharply. The pulling twisted her collar and she let out a strangled "Eurkk!" That wasn't a pincer holding on to her, it was a hand. She was being dragged down the corridor. The soles of her shoes squeaked against the floor. With a wriggling shrug she pulled herself loose and stood up.

The hand belonged to George. He flipped his tangled mass of hair out of his eyes in time to see that Twinkle was less than five metres behind them.

"Moooove!" he yelled.

He grabbed Sophie's arm and they belted for the stairs. Twinkle slashed a few hundred kilos out of the roof, which crashed at their heels. He bellowed angrily as they hurled themselves through the double doors above the stairwell.

They leapt down the cold stone stairs six at a time. Each jump sent a painful jolt through their legs, which almost made them lose their balance. Behind them, the double doors exploded outwards. They heard wood being ripped apart and pincers clacking. They didn't look back.

"It's you Twinkle's after," gasped George. "You've got to get out, draw him away from the others. Honestly, I'm surprised you hadn't realized that already."

Sophie's protest was interrupted by everything crumbling to rubble all around her. Twinkle stamped another dozen stairs to pieces. The wall beside them shifted and cracked.

They shot out of the building followed closely by chunks of stone and sections of metal banisters. The stone and banisters were followed closely by Twinkle.

Outside, the rest of the school was running about and howling even more than those inside. On any other day, this would have seemed perfectly normal, but now the staff were hiding in the library instead of joining in, so things were clearly worse than usual.

Julian, Dennis Biggs and the Great Projecto held on to the corner of the Science Block in an effort to avoid being caught in a stampede of sixth-formers. They and George had followed Twinkle's trail of bent lampposts and crushed pavements from the theatre to the school. Another performer, the Amazing Man of Nerves, had accompanied them, but he'd quickly burst into tears and been sent home.

"Over there!" called Julian above the din. "Across the sports fields!"

George gave him a lightning thumbs-up sign as he raced past. Sophie just gave him a hard stare. Twinkle didn't pay him the slightest attention. Not that Julian noticed any of it, since he was already hiding behind Dennis. Who was hiding behind the Great Projecto.

George and Sophie hurtled out across the football pitch. Twinkle's pincers snapped millimetres behind Sophie's head. Sophie's head kept telling Sophie's feet to bloomin' well get a move on.

"Why does it want meeeee?" she wailed.

"You're making him hungry," gasped George. "Let's see now. Do you smell funny?"

"NO!"

"Is your lower intestine filled with raw meat?"

"NO!"

"Are you wearing peach or strawberry flavoured clothes?"

"NO!"

"Beats me, then."

With an almighty, screeching roar, Twinkle

bounded over their heads and skidded to a halt in the penalty box. His claws dug into the grass. He crouched, coiling himself up, ready to spring. His eyes glinted brightly.

Trembling, Sophie pulled the packet of Squeezi-Mints from her pocket. "All I've got are these!"

Twinkle suddenly looked up with a hiss. George snatched the Squeezi-Mints and hurled them with every last molecule of energy he had. Twinkle sprang. His teeth closed on the mints in mid-air. He dropped to the ground chewing and snorting, shaking his head and spraying spit in all directions.

"Do you always carry those around with you?" said George, flopping into a muddy patch.

"Not any more," said Sophie. She wanted to flop too, but was unable to find a sufficiently mud-less patch.

Julian and the others came bounding over to them. They all grinned with relief, but kept a wary eye on Twinkle all the same. The monster was chewing away happily, licking the last of the Squeezi-Mints off his teeth. He was already sniffing around for more.

"Superb performance, young sir," cried Julian. "Worthy of the deep-sea scorpion-tamer whose boots I used to polish when I was Head Waiter at the Cosmic Cabaret Café. And you, dear girl, were bravery itself! Fearlessness unmatched by even the Ice Maidens of Greel, who have to undergo an ordeal of name-calling whenever there's a 'p' in the month! How can I – blugg—"

He'd blugged because George had grabbed hold of the lapels of his coat with one hand, while pointing at Twinkle with the other. Twinkle was rapidly vanishing into the distance, heading for the hedges on the far side of the sports fields. "For the last time, Julian. Where! Did! You! Get! Him!"

"Yes, that's what we'd all like to know," said the Great Projecto loftily.

"Oh, NOW his highness is getting all worried," said Dennis, doing a silly weedy-drippy dance. "Now it's too late. Now the thing's got out. Ooooo, ooooo."

The Great Projecto knocked him off his feet with one blow. "It wouldn't have escaped if YOU had used the extra restraints, as I told you, BIGGS."

They kicked and scratched in the mud. George tightened his grip on Julian.

"Well?" he demanded.

"Well, they're very bad boys aaaand ... they're out of tonight's show," said Julian.

"Not them. THAT thing tearing up hedges over there!"

Julian smiled weakly. "Well, ah, yes, I suppose, in the circumstances, all things being equal, what with one thing and another... But then look on the bright side. Think of the marvellous publicity we'll get."

"*Where?*" said George quietly. "*Did? You? Get him?*"

"At, umm, at our unscheduled stop at the refuelling station orbiting Neptune, I think. The details escape me. Such an insignificant, tiny incident. Ha haa. I had a meeting with an old colleague, a business associate you might say, and he, umm, he saw his way clear to doing me the most tremendous favour. Had this magnificent beast on special offer. What a pal, eh? A true friend is worth a thousand comedy dance routines, I always say."

"He sold him to you?"

"Ah, well, in this instance 'sold him' may not, strictly, be the exact words needed, at this point, so to speak. You see he ... what he sold me was the information I required in order to, umm ... take possession of our dear Twinkle over there. You know, security codes, access keys, that sort of thing."

George's eyes widened. "You ... *stole* Twinkle? Who from?"

"George, my lad, stealing is a very serious and terrible thing, and I'm hurt, deeply hurt, deeply deeply hurt, wounded to the very core—"

"Who from?"

"The Paxi. Anyway—"

George let go, as if Julian had suddenly become red hot. Dennis and the Great Projecto stopped fighting.

"Who are the Paxi?" said Sophie.

George flopped all over again. Dennis started to cry. The Great Projecto turned so pale he was almost transparent.

"Who are the Paxi?" said Sophie.

"Julian," shivered George, "are you MAD? Have you CASHED IN YOUR BRAIN at the local branch of Stupid Bank, or WHAT?"

"Weeeell," squirmed Julian. "There was a Paxi scout-ship docked at the station, and a quite enormous quantity of their crates and cages stored in Cargo Bay 6. Out of all those … well, one little… Don't look at me like that, George. We needed a star attraction, and don't you deny it."

George didn't deny it. His mind felt blank, and his stomach felt like it had gone on holiday to the far edge of space. Dennis started to whimper. The Great Projecto shut his eyes and prayed to St Gulpus, patron saint of theatricals in really awful trouble.

Twinkle had finished ripping up the last of the hedges. He bellowed impatiently, searching for something minty.

"Who are the Paxi?" said Sophie.

At that precise moment, the Paxi warship *Pulverizer* was 13 billion miles above her head, and closing.

CHAPTER FOUR

Extract from the next day's *Local Evening Telegraph*:

PERFORMERS PLACE
PUPILS IN PERIL

The town council held an emergency public meeting last night. Discussed was an incident staged at St Egbert's School by the staff of the new Galactic Coliseum theatre, recently built with National Lottery funds.

Councillors heard how high-tech Hollywood-style special-effects wizardry, taken from the show that's currently being staged, was used to destroy school property and terrify pupils, teachers and visitors. The school's headmaster told the meeting: "This kind of cheap publicity stunt is going too far! I demand an apology and a whacking great load of cash for new buildings! It didn't even fool me! I could tell it was a model!" Prominent local teacher Mrs Eileen Womsey urged those present to use their anger in a positive way. She reported that she would be encouraging her pupils to do a project on the power of advertising, to help them come to terms with their experience. One of her pupils, Wayne Banks, had earlier commented: "It was a bit boring. I could tell it was a cartoon." Rumours that the so-called creature is still at large should be laughed at, urged the council. There is no cause for alarm.

With a deep sigh, Sophie folded up the newspaper and dropped it into the kitchen swing-bin. "Amateurs," she mumbled. "A glass of water's got more depth than that report."

She made up her mind. She WOULD write a piece on the theatre. She would write about them, and expose them for the bunch of dangerous weirdos they were! And she might as well start right now!

She marched past the *ping … ping ping ping* noises coming from the study, out of the house, and across the field. It was another violently sunny day, and the tall bulk of the theatre threw a solid, squashed-rectangle shadow across the grass. The grass was ripped up in places, where Twinkle had passed by.

George had tried to lure the creature back to his cage with a trail of wafer-thin after-dinner choccies, but without success. Twinkle had followed the trail for barely a hundred metres. He'd smelt a faint whiff of more Squeezi-Mints coming from the south-west, and run off with a deafening roar. He had since ripped apart the Cosy Street Residential Home for Elderly Grannies. Eighty-two-year-old Mrs Sweetly had offered him a bag of fudge, but ninety-three-year-old Mrs Grumbleton would not let go of her jumbo Squeezi-Mint party pack. So he'd eaten her along with the Squeezi-Mints. Nobody knew where he was now, but alarming stories were coming from the area around Paradise Street and Murray Road.

George was currently busy removing the posters from the front of the theatre. Even though Sophie knew what a slob he was, the way he was ripping them down and letting the pieces flutter away on the breeze told her that he was in a hurry. Several of the backstage crew were nervously checking engine exhaust tubes and the guttering around the roof.

"A-hem!" said Sophie loudly. She had her notebook ready and her pen poised to write.

"Sorry," said George, without looking round. "In a bit of a rush."

"I demand to know the full story."

"The full story? We're leaving."

"There must be more to it than that," said Sophie.

"OK. We're leaving very quickly," said

George. Shreds of poster were collecting in his hair.

"Ever since yesterday, you people have simply clammed up. I want to know what's going on! I want to know what you're going to do about that rampaging monster! AND I WANT TO KNOW WHO THE PAXI ARE!"

One of the backstage crew nearly fell off his ladder. Another let out a high-pitched whine and stuck his head in a bucket. George winced and flapped his hand in a "Shhhh" motion. He hurried Sophie into the theatre's thickly carpeted foyer.

"They're upset enough as it is," he hissed. "Don't be insensitive."

Sophie fought back the urge to call him something very insensitive indeed. "These Paxi will be coming here soon, I take it? What will they do then?"

"Oh, I should think they'll take over this whole planet. Maybe they'll use it as a strategic base in their war with the Yaanians. Maybe they'll just blow it to bits."

Sophie's face got tangled up in itself for a moment. "Pardon?" she said at last. "W-Wh-What do we do?"

"Well, you'd better go and live somewhere else. Never mind, there are plenty of other planets about."

"But I want to live on THIS planet!"

"Sorry, it's doomed," said George, shrugging his shoulders. "Look, I hate to rush you, but I've got a lot to do, and we reckon the Paxi will be here about teatime, so..."

"H-H-How bad are they, exactly?"

George took a deep breath. "The Paxi are one of the most awful species you could meet in this dimension. They've been at war with the Yaanians for nearly six and a half thousand years, and the Yaanians are getting pretty fed up of it."

"The Yaanians?"

"Really nice people. Look a bit like swans, dress a bit like rock stars. They used to have a vast empire. Now they've mostly got a vast heap of muck and nothing."

"If they're so nice, why are they at war?" said Sophie.

"Once upon a time, there was a Paxi and a Yaanian living next door to each other. One day, the Paxi's pet slime-worm did a big poo on the Yaanian's lawn. They started arguing over the fence and the Paxi threw the poo through the Yaanian's window and ... it just kind of escalated."

"They're fighting over a poo?" cried Sophie.

George looked extremely serious. "A slime-worm poo," he said, as if she ought to know better than to ask a question like that. "They're very, very smelly."

"So what does Twinkle have to do with the Paxi?"

"Twinkle, I'd guess, is part of their weapons system. You see they... Shhh! Listen!"

The low whine they could hear might have been the theatre's engines being tested ready for takeoff. It might have been some of the backstage crew moaning about the Paxi. George and Sophie hoped, more than anything else in the world, that it WASN'T a giant spaceship landing outside. Some hope.

CHAPTER FIVE

Outside, the Paxi warship *Pulverizer* extended its three landing legs as it descended. It was a round, irregular-shaped dome, the size of a fairly important sports stadium. It was a faintly luminous, streaky-brown colour, and around its base whirred the magnetic discs which powered it. Turning slowly in mid-air, it finally settled about a hundred metres from the theatre. Its far edge scraped the chimney pots on Sophie's house.

A long, low opening appeared along the ship's side, out of which came a rubbery-looking ramp, followed by a line of rubbery-looking aliens. They wore dirty, studded body armour and waddled sloppily on webbed feet. Their erupting skin and bulging eyes would have made the world's ugliest toad bring up its breakfast. Their floppy, toothless mouths would have made the toad think twice about lunch too. With the membranes which covered their hands, they all shielded themselves from the warmth and the sunlight.

They had made swifter progress in finding Earth than George had estimated. This was thanks to the leaflets Julian had given out all over the Neptune refuelling station. The leaflets said: "Come and see our next spectacular show! Earth, co-ordinates X-345-2-P-11-Z! Only three days from this station (at warp 5)!"

George and Sophie ran out of the theatre just in time to see the backstage crew hurry off into the distance. The Paxi at the head of the line jammed a grubby, box-like helmet on his head and stepped down on to the grass with a heavy plop.

"I, Ix of the Hydrax League of the Paxi, Commander of the glorious vessel here landed, claim this planet and all that is upon it!" he spat in a globulous voice. He blinked painfully up at the cloudless sky for a moment. "FA!" he shouted. "FA!"

Fa of the Voxton League, his second in command, stepped forward. "I crave your orders, Commander!"

"Why is the climate-control unit not functioning?" demanded Ix. "This daylight is intolerable!"

"I have not ordered it to be unpacked yet, Commander."

"No excuses! You are inadequate!" cried Ix.

He pulled a small black sphere from the chest section of his armour and squeezed it. A whooping snap of purple energy shot out. Fa exploded in a splash of slime.

"What can we do to stop them?" whispered Sophie. The ghastly smell that leaked from their bodies had started duffing up her nose. She quickly blocked her nostrils with the back of her hand.

"We can't stop them," said George. "All we can do is run away. Come on!"

They ran. And they ran. Ix was used to having people run away from him, and took no notice. He issued orders on more important matters instead.

"Unpack the climate-control unit and set at maximum. Seal off the immediate area. Round up the local population. And BRING ME THE HUMAN JULIAN CHIMES TO FACE PUNISHMENT!"

It took the Paxi less than five Earth minutes to overrun the theatre. The few performers and backstage crew who hadn't already left by the fire exit were found hiding under the make-up table. Julian was read a list of his crimes against the mighty and glorious Paxi plan of galactic conquest. Strictly speaking, he'd only committed *one* crime by stealing Twinkle, but the Paxi accused him of another thirty-six anyway, just to make sure. Then he was hauled off to a cell on the *Pulverizer*.

A herd of twelve Twinkles which the Paxi had brought with them was set free, to terrorize the neighbourhood. They quickly met up with the original Twinkle, who showed them his favourite sweet shop and all the best places in town to stamp on.

Sophie's house was ransacked as soon as the first wave of Paxi warriors had finished ripping up half the seats in the theatre. Sophie's dad managed to hang on to his piano for almost thirty seconds before the Paxi got fed up of pulling him by his legs, and simply smashed the piano to bits instead. He was dragged out of the house with his cardigan wrapped around his head and a dozen piano keys gripped in each fist. He was so angry at being interrupted, he hadn't noticed that the Paxi were foul-smelling amphibians from outer space. Muffled cries about music critics and legal action came from inside the cardigan as it bounced over the front step.

Meanwhile, Commander Ix supervised the invasion of the town. Telephone and power lines were cut. A jamming signal from the warship blotted out all radio and TV transmissions for a 10-mile radius. Paxi patrolled the streets. People were flushed out of shops and offices by roaming Twinkles, and zapped unconscious by warriors with chest weapons set to stun. They were then carried back to an enormous enclosure being set up in the field next to the spaceship.

This enclosure was completely escape-proof and surrounded by a high fence. The Paxi liked to call it the Hospitality Area. Inside, electronic food dispensers were nailed to posts here and there. Commander Ix had years of experience in bringing misery into the lives of other species, so he made sure that all the food dispensers only served things that nobody liked. He also made sure that the tents provided as shelter came with no instructions about how to put them up.

Ix had his specially moulded armchair brought from his cabin and placed right on top of the ship. He nestled into its cool squishiness, watching the invasion begin and spitting orders into the communicator clamped to his cheek. Speakers either side of his chair warbled out his favourite Paxi pop songs, very loudly. The local citizens dumped in the Hospitality Area woke up to blinding headaches and, echoing around them, boppy poppy tunes which sounded like a choir of distressed pigs.

Meanwhile, black pods like inflated dustbin liners were carried from the ship, each growing in a tub of soil. They were replanted all around the outer edge of the town, in gardens, on grass verges, or on waste ground. They grew quickly and steadily, greedily slurping up nutrients through their roots, waiting to play their part in the invasion...

While all this was going on, the climate-control unit was set up. It was a metallic device, about thirty metres high, studded at odd intervals with circular lumps and craters. Once it was switched on, a dim, pulsing light seemed to drift around its insides. High above it, clouds began to form. They were wispy at first, then thicker and blacker. Soon it began to rain.

About half a kilometre from the *Pulverizer*, George and Sophie were hiding behind the counter of the Fragrant Harbour.

"Rain!" said Sophie, watching the first drips zigzag down the window. "That's all we need. The forecast said we'd have sunshine till the end of the week."

"That's got nothing to do with the forecast," said George. "That'll be the Paxi turning the town into something more suitable for them. Their climate-control units are the best in the galaxy. Built to last, too."

Sophie didn't like the sound of that, but she'd had one too many shocks already that day. She pretended she hadn't heard. She also pretended not to hear the RGRRRRAAAs, FSS-ZAPPs and AHHRGHHHs coming from outside. More people were being rounded up in front of the newsagent's down the street.

The Fragrant Harbour was dark and deserted. The back door was open. On top of the counter goldfish swam lazily around a gently bubbling tank. If the fish were as scared, tired and confused as George and Sophie, they didn't let on.

George had found an old power cell amongst the junk in his pockets and had discharged enough heat into the floor to keep the Paxi away for a while. But already the room was starting to cool down. George checked the cell's tiny readout. "Not much juice left in this thing," he mumbled. "Better save it, just in case."

Sophie was sure her mum would have been caught by now. Mum had said she'd be spending the day closing down a factory on the industrial estate next to the park. That was only a couple of miles away. George was thinking along similar lines.

"Did you see them get Douglas the android? He's strong as an ox and clever as a bagful of brains. If they've got him, they're bound to have Julian. He's weak as a kitten and daft as a concrete hat."

"Wait!" cried Sophie. "I know! I know! You could organize a song and dance number featuring the entire cast and distract the Paxi, and then when they're looking the other way we could blow up their ship and ... and...! And we'd be OK! It's a mad idea but it might just work!"

"Saaaay, you're right!" said George sarcastically. "It IS a mad idea."

Sophie's face drooped, and she curled up, hugging her knees. She thought about a couple of the reports she'd written for the school newspaper recently: "Canteen Crisis: Sausage Shortage Shock!" and "Staff-Room Source Leaks Headmaster's Memo: Classroom Discipline To Be Tightened!" They seemed distant and pointless compared to today's news.

"I'm sorry," she said quietly. "I'm too upset to think straight."

George shuffled uncomfortably. "Look... I didn't mean to ... it's just that... Oh quasars, I don't have any more idea of what to do than you. The only thing that would make the Paxi leave now is the destruction of their climate-control unit, and frankly that's not possible."

Water was pouring down the window in torrents now. Puddles were deepening and spreading out across the road. Rumbles of thunder rolled across the sky. George came to a decision.

"However, what IS possible is me getting off this planet," he said. He stood up and marched out into the rain. Sophie followed, but paused in the doorway. No umbrella! No coat! She pulled her collar up as far as it would go, tucked her hands tightly into her armpits, and tiptoed after him. She skipped around the puddles and hurried between whatever patches of shelter she could find.

"You can't leave!" she called. "What about Julian, and Douglas, and Dennis, and everyone!"

"I'm not responsible for them!" said George. The rain had already turned his hair into a twisted splat on top of his head. "They can take care of themselves! None of this is my fault!"

"The whole town is being captured. We have to do something!"

"I *am* doing something. I'm going back to the theatre, I'm resetting the engines, and I'm off." George marched on.

Sophie's squeak of anger was lost in the sound of the rain. "That is complete, utter, total selfishness!"

George stopped marching on. "No," he said. "That is sensible, life-preserving, positive action."

"But it's Julian's theatre! You'd be stealing it, just like he stole Twinkle!"

"I think he's got more important things to think about. If the Paxi have got him, they'll be putting him on trial. And if he's put on trial by the Paxi, he'll need the most brilliant defence lawyer in the entire universe if he's going to avoid being neutralized!"

Exactly the same thought had occurred to Julian the moment he'd been caught. That's why he'd chosen the brainiest person he knew to be his lawyer. While George and Sophie were busy arguing, a Paxi warrior was fetching the brainiest person Julian knew from the Hospitality Area.

"Step forward, Douglas the android!" bellowed the warrior. His name was Ko (of the Pholpon League), and he hated being on legal duty. The Hospitality Area's captives were assembled in front of him.

Sophie's mum leapt from the crowd. "That's me!" she squealed. "My name's Douglas! I demand you remove me from this disgusting place! I have an appointment at five-thirty!"

Ko looked her up and down with his bulbous eyes. "You are not an android."

The rest of the crowd yelled out that THEY were androids, and started doing jerky dances and looking unemotional to prove it. Ko sighed. He'd told his supervisor that they should have liquidated the humans as soon as they'd landed. But, oooh no, his supervisor wouldn't listen. His supervisor was sooo sure they'd be useful for something.

"Shut up, you useless lot!" he ordered. They shut up. He waded into the crowd, pushing people out of the way as he went. They moved to avoid him, but he pushed them anyway. The rain was rapidly turning the field beneath his feet into sticky mud. For a moment, it made him feel homesick. He quickly told himself not to be such a pathetic weakling, and pushed the humans harder to make up for it.

He grabbed Douglas (who'd given himself away by being the only one not making a fuss) and dragged him away. Douglas barely managed to hold on to the cardboard box full of bits he used in his robot-folding act. Ko glared at the people who scurried along beside them.

"I shall be writing to my MP about this!" said the headmaster.

"Can't we be friends?" said Mrs Womsey. "Perhaps we could all sit down and discuss our feelings."

"Let him go," cried Dennis and the Great Projecto. "He's our best act!"

The gate in the Hospitality Area's high fence clanged shut in their faces. Ko slung Douglas over his shoulder and stalked off into the spaceship. From behind the gate came feeble, pleading cries of "Help!", "You heartless, uncaring fiends!" and "How do we put these tents up, then?"

Meanwhile, deep inside the warship, Julian was practising some feeble, pleading cries of his own. Perhaps if he grovelled and wept enough, Commander Ix might take pity on him? Perhaps if he held the court spellbound with the moving saga of his performance of *Hamlet* at the Asteroid Starhouse, he could get away with only having to clean the toilets for a while?

"Fat chance," he murmured.

A round hatch above him suddenly buzzed open. In a second, his tiny cell turned itself inside out through the hatch. He was pushed up into the courtroom, and the inside-out cell moulded itself into an oozing mound on which he could sit. He chose to stand.

The courtroom was shadowy and evil-smelling. Like the rest of the Paxi ship, its walls, floor and ceiling were damp and lumpy. Dark lines snaked around them, like veins beneath skin, and they gave off a dim, eerie light. Commander Ix stood on a squelchy area raised up from the rest of the room. A gang of warriors squatted behind Julian. They didn't need to be there, they just enjoyed seeing different species suffer.

Ko entered, dumped Douglas (and his cardboard box) at Julian's feet, and saluted Commander Ix. "Council for the Defence has been acquired, Commander! The trial may proceed!"

"I'm so glad you're here, Douglas old chap," burbled Julian. "Choose someone to defend you, they said, and instantly you sprang to mind. Your calmness under pressure! Your fierce intelligence! Your cool android logic will soon slice through the twisted lies they—"

"Belt up!" yelled Ko. He slapped his fist on the floor three times as a signal that the trial was under way. He cleared his throat, which for a Paxi meant making a noise like half an ocean being squirted through a sieve.

"Julian Chimes of Earth," he cried. "In the presence of our supreme leader, and as Council for the Attack, I hereby accuse you of grievous crimes against our noble battle fleet. These crimes being..." He pulled a crumpled roll of paper from inside his uniform. It unwound in a long, spiralling heap. "These crimes being many and various. But basically, you nicked one of our monsters. How do you plead, a bit guilty or completely guilty?"

The gang of warriors growled and slapped their lips. Commander Ix held up a hand for silence.

"I'm... I'm not guilty at all," shuddered Julian.

The warriors growled louder. Ix leaned forward. "Irrelevant!" he gurgled. "You are accused. Therefore you are guilty. Your Council for the Defence will now beg for forgiveness and mercy!"

Julian nudged Douglas. "You're on," he hissed. "Knock their socks off, kiddo. Outwit them with some brilliant line of legal reasoning. Show 'em what your superior android brain can achieve."

Douglas stepped forward. Julian held his breath.

Douglas pulled on a pair of white gloves. He held up his hands. He looked around the courtroom, smiling politely. Then he rummaged in his cardboard box. Two minutes later, he'd assembled a robot of Commander Ix. It stepped forward and took a bow. "Ta daa," it said, in a tinny voice. Douglas bowed too.

"Thanks ever so," said Julian quietly. Ko crushed the robot with a single blow.

"Case proven!" spat Ix. The warriors cheered. "Julian Chimes of Earth, you are an enemy of the Paxi. Standard invasion procedure says that all enemies must die. You will be taken from this place to a really uncomfortable cell. At 92:45a.m., Paxon mean time, you will be publicly neutralized. You will suffer the Torment of a Thousand Nibbles. Take him away!"

Two of the warriors took an arm and a leg each. He put up no resistance, so they shook him about a bit to make things more fun. Douglas was dragged back to the Hospitality Area.

"You have no proof!" wailed Julian shakily. "You have no evidence! How can you know it was me?"

"You were caught on the security camera!" said Ix. "You left DNA traces all over the place! AND I had everyone on that refuelling station thumped until they said they personally had seen you do it! Hah!"

"It's a fair cop," sobbed Julian, as they

carried him off. "But you won't get away with this! You can't use me as an excuse to invade yet another planet! The brave people of Earth will defend themselves to the very end. They'll send missiles and aircraft. With heroic courage in their hearts and steely determination in their eyes, they'll win through! They'll triumph against the odds! And then you'll be nobbled, sunshine!"

Julian was right and wrong. He was right about the missiles and the aircraft. He was wrong about everything else.

At the same moment as he was being hurled into the most uncomfortable cell he'd ever been hurled into, a squadron of jet fighters was approaching the town. Night was now falling, as well as rain. The pilots of the jet fighters switched their displays to "See in the Dark" mode. They thought they'd come to the wrong place, because instead of a park there was a steaming swamp. Instead of busy streets there were deserted buildings. The movements of weird creatures kept setting off the alarms on their radars.

The pilots never even noticed the black pods. These had been growing and spreading their roots ever since they were replanted around the edge of the town during the first stage of the invasion. Now they were enormous, and wrinkly. Their tops uncurled like the petals of flowers as the aircraft flew over-

73

head. As soon as they sensed something in the sky above them …

ThHHHHHAAPPPPPPPPPSSSSssss

… stinging tendrils, thousands of metres long, shot upwards from inside them. The electrified tips of the tendrils slapped around the aircraft, fusing their guidance systems and sending them plunging into the swamp. The pilots ejected, only to be zapped unconscious by patrolling Paxi warriors the minute they hit the ground.

Twenty minutes later, a volley of missiles was aimed at the Paxi ship. They had "Get this, alien nasties" and "Earthlings are brill" chalked along their sides. As they swooped down at their target, the stinger pods wrapped their tendrils around them and pulled them into their leafy stomachs. The missiles were fully digested in about an hour. Earth's defences decided to give up and surrender.

All night, warriors patrolled the town in large groups. There was no need to, because nearly all the locals were now in the Hospitality Area, arguing about how to put the tents up. The warriors patrolled in search of fun. They worked their way along rows of houses, seeing who could blast them apart with the fewest energy zaps. They painted rude words in long, curvy lines on the sides of abandoned cars. They stuffed any cats they found into a big sack, ready for a tasty fry-up at suppertime.

Back at the warship, Commander Ix snuggled down into the warm mushiness of his bed. Before he ordered the light to turn itself off, he sent a message back to the Paxi's home planet. It read:

To: **His Overwhelming Presidency, Supreme War Council, Bunker 19B**
Dear Lord of the Seven Worlds
• Property regained.
• Criminal element to be crushed in the morning.
• Invasion phase 1 complete.
Base location established. Will send signal soon, when ready to receive battle fleet. Planet found to be suitable for new fortress in magnificent war of death against Yaanian scum.
Love to Zi and the kids,
Ix
In Command
Warship Pulverizer

CHAPTER SIX

Sophie's room was filled with weird shadows, cast by the glow of the spaceship outside her window. The electricity supply had been cut, but they dared not switch on a torch for fear of being spotted. George discharged the last of the heat from the power cell into the wall. It was lucky that the cell was almost empty, because the wallpaper instantly began to smoulder.

If the Paxi hadn't placed motion-sensing security floodlights all around the theatre, George would have been halfway to Mars by now. Sophie felt relieved that he wasn't. She hated herself for feeling relieved, but George seemed to be the only person not captured by the Paxi who knew anything about them. Therefore, he was the only person who was likely to come up with a plan of action. The thought of having to actually RELY on the obnoxious pig made her want to be sick.

She quickly scribbled another page of notes in the A4 jotter pad on her desk. She'd had a few ideas on how to write up her exclusive, on-the-spot report about the invasion.

"Could have been halfway to Mars by now," said George, peeping at the warship over the windowsill. He snorted a couple of times, and cleaned out his nose with his sleeve. "I expect they'll be letting out the swamp snakes soon. Now it's dark."

Sophie closed her eyes for a moment. She thought calm thoughts, about mowing the back lawn and carefully clipping it around the edges. "Ottershaw Faces Test Of Nerves," she whispered to herself. "I'm like a war correspondent. Keeping a cool head in the face of danger. I could even write a book about all this, when it's over… If I live that long."

"Wow, books!" cried George. Sophie opened her eyes. He was pulling paperbacks off her shelves at random, flicking through, and jamming them back in completely the wrong order.

"Stop it!" she squeaked.

"You've got a whole library of them here! I've only got three. You can't really get books outside this sector of space. Well, not in any language I can read, anyway. I've had one called *Pinky Pixie and the Elephants* since I was tiny, but that's kind of lost its magic now.

Wooooowww. Can I have them?"

"NO!"

"Can I have some of them?"

"NO! Look, time's running out. You said yourself they'll send Julian for neutralization in the morning. We've got to do something, George! There are terrible things going on out there, and they have to be dealt with!"

George looked thoughtful. Sophie reckoned that at last she was getting through to him. He paced around the room for a few moments, then came to a definite decision. He snapped his fingers.

"Can I BUY some of them?"

Sophie took a deep breath. "You can ... borrow ... one ... if you must."

George grinned and pulled a "yippee" face. He chose a thick volume of short stories and quickly wedged it inside his overalls. Sophie also came to a definite decision.

"Well, if you haven't got the guts to help sort things out," she said, "then I bloomin' well have! So much for having to actually RELY on you." She turned to leave. "I wish you WERE halfway to Mars," she added, "you're no use to anyone here!"

George suddenly looked up at her. Then he looked at the warship. Then he looked at Sophie again. "What are you going to do?" he asked.

"I'm going inside that ship, and I'm going to

78

rescue Julian, and I'm going to find a way to destroy the climate-control unit and stop the invasion."

"You don't stand a chance," he said, his eyebrows raised as high as they could go.

She stalked over to him and prodded him in the chest. "Better-than-not-trying-at-all!"

That made him angry. If there was one thing he couldn't stand, it was being prodded in the chest. "Right!" he announced. "Let's go, then! And when we're captured, and pushed around really roughly, and sent back to the Paxi homeworld as domestic servants, don't say I didn't warn you!"

"Told you it'd be a doddle," whispered George.

He'd thrown a stone at the theatre. The floodlights had blinked on. The guards around the ramp leading up to the warship had scuttled over to investigate. Now George and Sophie were crouched at the top of the ramp. Apart from the splashes of light around the theatre, it was pitch-dark. The sounds of bickering and clanking tent poles drifted over from the Hospitality Area. In front of them was the long, low door leading into the ship.

"Quick!" hissed Sophie. "The guards will be back any second, they're not THAT daft!" She peered at the door through the gloom. "Have you got some sort of skeleton key? Is there an entry code we've got to crack?"

"No, you press this squeezy thing here."
He pressed it. The door slid back silently.
Sophie looked surprised.

"They don't lock them," said George in a
didn't-you-know-that? voice. "Who'd be stupid enough to sneak on to a Paxi warship?"

They hurried inside. The door slid shut
behind them, and resealed itself with green
ooze around the edges. They were in a narrow,
dimly lit corridor which curved out of sight to
the left. Sophie stared in horror at the lumpy
surfaces and the gently pulsing glow that was
inside everything around them.

"Eugh," she said.

"These ships aren't built, they're grown,"
whispered George. "I guess this corridor
would be the equivalent of a windpipe."

"Oh thank you for telling me," hissed
Sophie. "I feel so much better knowing that."

She stepped carefully on the uneven floor.
The risk of tripping over and touching something kept her mind off the greater dangers
of the situation. They crept along the corridor. Sophie took out her notebook and pen.
Then she decided that her handwriting
would be too shaky to read, so she put them
back again.

"Julian will be somewhere nearby," whispered George. "Saves a long walk to the neutralization area outside."

"There doesn't seem to be anyone about.

Perhaps they're all asleep."

"That's against regulations," said George. "Only officers are allowed to sleep. It's fifty smacks on the leg with a stick if you nod off on duty. And if you have an afternoon nap you get melted down into liquid fertilizer."

"Charming. Where are they all then?"

"In there," said George quietly. He pointed to a ragged gap in the wall, through which an ugly warbling sound was coming. They peeped in.

A hundred Paxi warriors were slumped around an enormous circular room which looked as though *it* had been caught having an afternoon nap. In the middle of them was Ko of the Pholpon League. He was concluding his lecture entitled "Efficient Use of a 90,000-Volt Pain Cube" with a rousing song to boost morale and help the war effort. George and Sophie were in time to hear the last verse:

> *So crush the Yaanian foe, my friends,*
> *And hurl them into space,*
> *And if a Yaanian smiles at you*
> *Hit him in the face.*
> *There's good times up ahead, my friends,*
> *We'll smash the universe*
> *And once we've ruined everything*
> *We'll go and do something worse! Oi!*

"My name's Ko, thank you and goodnight."

81

The warriors clapped and whistled.

"Surely," gasped Sophie, "if the Yaanians are as nice as you say, they'd offer these wretched horrors a peace treaty or something?"

"Oh they do, regularly," whispered George. "On expensive paper, with flowery lettering on and everything. The Paxi usually wipe their bottoms on it. Which is an improvement, I suppose, 'cos normally they don't bother wiping their bottoms at all."

"Haven't these people done *anything* good? Haven't they got *anything* they can be proud of, anything they've actually *achieved*?"

"No," said George. "When little baby Paxi crawl out of their egg sacs, the first thing they're taught to say is 'Death to all Yaanians, no mercy, not even if they beg'. Then they get chucked in a tank of mutant killer fish to toughen them up. It's no wonder they grow up nasty."

Ko bowed, and acknowledged the warriors' applause. Many of them had tears in their eyes. The rest of them had lumps in their throats. They shook their tears and lumps on to the floor and began to disperse.

"Yikes!" said George. "Meeting's over! They're coming this way!"

George and Sophie rushed for the temporary safety of the shadows. Squelching footsteps approached the gap in the wall. George grabbed Sophie's arm and they hurried further along the corridor, moving deeper and deeper into the ship. The squelching, and the sound of moist voices, followed them.

The further they went, the dimmer the light seemed to become. Sophie was convinced that the warping glow in the walls was following them too.

They passed a row of circular hatches set into the ceiling. In the centre of each hatch was a transparent plastic panel. George scurried back and forth between them, craning his neck to see what was inside.

"Empty... Empty... Sand slug. Oh, charming! And you, mate... Empty... Here!"

Julian's face was pressed flat against the plastic. George jumped, but couldn't reach the release switch next to the hatch.

"Quick!" he said to Sophie, signalling for her to cup her hands. "Gimme a leg up!"

Sophie glanced at the filthy state of George's shoes. "No," she said, "you lift me."

The footsteps were getting closer. Long, moving shadows rippled along the corridor behind them.

Sophie clambered up to kneel on George's shoulders. She stretched upwards as far as she could. Not quite far enough. George heaved her up by her knees. Her knuckles squashed against the release switch. With a squeal, she dropped to the floor. With a hiss of air, the hatch dropped open. With a "wooaaa", Julian dropped on top of them.

"George!" he cried.

"Shhh!" said George.

"And the delightful Miss Ottershaw! What a sight for sore eyes, and indeed sore legs. Never before have I been confined in such an uncomfortable place. I swear the damp has soaked clean through my sinuses."

"Shhh!" said Sophie. "The Paxi are right behind us."

Julian glanced over their shoulders. He tried to put on a brave face, but only managed a frightened and wobbly one. "We must fly!" he gulped. "Oh, how can I ever repay your kindness, my friends? I was a fool, trapped by my wanton desire for fame and fortune. I tripped over in my reckless dash along life's rocky road, and fell right in the doo-doo. But you came to save me anyway! Such courage, such faithfulness!"

"Yeh yeh yeh," grumbled George. "Come ON! If you stop yacking for half a second we might just have time to get—"

Caught. Warriors blocked the corridor behind them. Slobbery smiles wriggled across their faces. One of them gurgled into his communicator for reinforcements. Ko, out in front, licked his thin lips and folded his arms. He swayed from side to side, chuckling.

"Now then, humans," he said in a kindly voice. "I am Ko of the Pholpon League, and

I'll be your enemy for this evening. How would you like to die? Boiled in raw lizard grease or fired into the air as targets for shooting practice? You choose. We don't mind either way."

The warriors giggled. Julian felt a sudden urge to go to the toilet.

"Correct me if I'm wrong," whispered Sophie. "I'm only guessing here. But this is where we run for our lives, right?"

"RIGHT!" shouted George.

The three of them turned and fled. At that moment, they still had the merest, teeny-tiny drop of hope tucked away in the back of their minds. They had no idea what was up ahead.

"Shall we give them a ten-second start, lads?" said Ko. "Make it more fun."

The warriors giggled and dribbled. Then they made the official Paxi war cry of "PaKkAAAAAAAA!" The thunderous sound reverberated along the corridor. George, Sophie and Julian started yelling to stop themselves falling over in fear.

Hopping and waddling with excitement, the warriors rushed after them. The front rank squeezed their chest weapons. Twisting bolts of energy bounced off the walls. The top millimetre of George's hair vaporized in a shower of sparks. The right shoulder of Julian's coat was instantly shredded into loose fibres.

The warriors fired again. What with energy

bolts and war cries and George, Sophie and Julian yelling (in between dodging energy bolts), the noise in the corridor was deafening.

George didn't normally do a lot of running. He wasn't sure how much longer he could keep going at this speed. Sophie had been in the school's athletics team the year before, but even she was beginning to get tired. They both wished that something would turn up so that they could catch their breath for a moment or two. Seconds later, when something did turn up, they both wished it hadn't.

The voice of one of the warriors rose above the noise. "The humans are in the target area, sir!"

"Activate!" cried Ko.

Suddenly a long section of floor beneath George, Sophie and Julian dissolved. They dropped for what seemed like a hundred metres. All three of them were knocked unconscious. The floor solidified again above their heads, cutting off the sound of the warriors' laughter.

A strange nothingness buzzed through their heads until they awoke. They stood up slowly, rubbing their bruises. They couldn't see a thing.

"Oh my stars! I've gone blind!"

"Shut up, Julian, there's just no light in here," said George.

"Where is here?" groaned Sophie.

Whatever this place was, it was warm and musty-smelling. The occasional plink of a water droplet came from somewhere over there. The slight echo of their voices told them that the space around them was large.

"Hhhhhhhh…"

Each assumed that this "hhhhhhhh" was one of the others breathing a bit funnily. None of them said anything for a few moments. Each assumed they were the only one getting a weird crawly feeling.

"They're … they're keeping us locked up for a while … yes?" said Sophie quietly.

"I … dunno," said George.

"Ssssssssssssssssssss…"

"Julian! Don't be disgusting!"

"That's not me, old boy. Scout's honour. I think it came from that direction. Or maybe that direction."

"Where's that direction? I can't see you, can I?" said George.

"HhhhhaaaaSSSsssssssssssss…"

"Oh. That direction. Right," said George. His voice was trembling like a jelly on a spring.

Sophie heard something heavy shifting along behind her. She jumped forward and fell, disoriented by the blackness. She pressed her hands flat against the smooth, clammy floor. Was she in the middle of this place? Or at one side? Or on the very edge of a bottomless pit?

"HhhhSSSSSSSSSSSSSss…"

It was very close to her. Whatever it was.

"What time is it?" said George, in a voice so low Sophie could barely hear him.

"Can't see my watch," breathed Sophie. "Past midnight, anyway."

"Either the Paxi are late letting them out or they've kept them in especially. To deal with us."

"Kept what in?" whispered Sophie.

For a moment there was silence. Total silence.

"Swamp snakes," whispered George.

"WOOAAAAHHHHHH!" screamed Julian. "Swamp snakes!" He staggered backwards and collided with Sophie.

"HAhhhhssssSSSSSSsssss   …   sssss-saaaaaaa…"

"Bu-wh-ca—" stammered Sophie.

George's voice could scarcely be heard. "The Paxi normally let them loose after midnight. Swamp snakes are their night watchmen." The plinking of water seemed to be getting closer. Julian babbled and muttered.

"I hate snakes," shivered Sophie. "Twisty, wriggly things."

"Swamp snakes don't wriggle," whispered George. "They're about forty metres long."

Sophie's fists tightened. Her nails dug painfully into her palms. "C-Can they see us? In the dark?"

"They have no eyes," whispered George. "They have a sort of soft disc on the top of their head. It senses movement. Stay ... still ... and ... keep ... as quiet ... as possible..."

Sophie held her breath. Her legs were shaking. Don't move! The shaking got worse. Stop it! Stop it! Don't MOVE!

Something large slithered beside her. Something heavy. A hard, scaly surface brushed against her arm.

It was all too much for Julian. With a howl that any werewolf would have been proud of, he leapt up and ran in whatever direction happened to take his fancy. Huge, sliding bodies suddenly started to move quickly all around them.

"Julian!" spat George. "Pack it in! You'll get us all eaten!"

"I'll never do bad things again!" sobbed Julian at the top of his voice.

The sliding got faster. A low, wheezy hiss seemed to come from all directions at once.

George and Sophie stood their ground as best they could. The massive bulk of the snakes nudged them off balance one way, then the other. The writhing circle around them was getting smaller.

"They'll crush us," breathed George.

"Where's Julian?" whispered Sophie.

"W W w w w A A A A A A A A A H A H A - H A H H H !"

"Oh, there he is," said George.

Julian felt a hot, rumbling breeze across his face. He suddenly realized that a gaping mouth was directly above his head. On a wetting-your-pants scale of 1 to 10, he hit 163. He dived to one side, and slapped into a wall of flesh.

"W W w w w A A A A A A A A A H A H A - H A H H H !"

George and Sophie leapt up and clambered over the backs of ... two snakes? Three? The snakes reared and twisted. George and Sophie were thrown heels over head. They landed against something that gave an echoing clang.

"Could be the exit tube!" gasped George. "Quick! Feel for a release switch, like the one on Julian's cell!"

A snake's tail slammed into him. Sophie heard a whoosh-bang as he was flipped back against a nearby bulkhead.

"George!"

No answer.

"Julian?"

No answer. Julian tried to call out, "The switch, dear girl! Save us all from the deadly coils of these monstrous serpents!", but he couldn't. He was too busy being crushed by the coils of these monstrous serpents himself.

A sudden shudder from one of the snakes pushed Sophie over. She crawled along on her knees. In the darkness, her hands groped blindly across the wall. She found a rough, cir-cular bump. With a leaping heart, she hit it.

Nothing happened. That wasn't the switch.

She searched up as high as she could stretch. Everything felt smooth.

A great weight suddenly jammed her against the wall. She squealed in pain, and as she did so, the snake's scales pressed harder.

Then her fingers found a dent in the wall. There was a shuddering lurch, and everything dropped away beneath her feet.

CHAPTER SEVEN

Out in the open air, three swamp snakes slapped into the rain-soaked mud in front of the spaceship. A human female fell out beside them and slid into a deep puddle. One of the snakes had two human males wrapped in its coils.

Sheets of lightning flashed through the thick clouds overhead. The snakes roared, as if in answer to the air-shattering bangs of thunder. Jagged red and black patterns rippled down their sides. On top of their wide, flat heads, the discs George had described to Sophie stood like mohican haircuts. The lower halves of their heads hinged loosely to form enormous jaws.

Two of them instantly sensed distant, interesting movement – the rolling of barrels which had spilled out from an abandoned lorry on the road beyond Sophie's house. They slithered away to investigate, undulating in wide S shapes, carving curvy trenches in the boggy earth beneath them. The third snake decided to make a meal of its two captives first.

Sophie spluttered to her feet, dripping with mud. Julian was on the point of losing consciousness. Almost every molecule of breath had been crushed out of him. George wasn't far behind.

"Sophie," he wheezed. The snake shifted to get a better grip. "Tear off ... its ... disc..."

WHAT? Sophie was caught between the horror of what was happening to George and Julian, and the horror of what George was suggesting. There was the disc, on top of the snake's head. It was shiny, and about the same size as a Frisbee.

As another clap of thunder shook the sky, the snake wrapped itself into a tighter knot. Julian slumped forward. All George could do was pull a face. The snake's head swung low, ready to slide up and chew its prey at leisure.

This was no time to be squeamish. Sophie steadied herself for a moment, then jumped on to the snake's neck with a loud "Yaaaa!"

Instantly the snake reared up, its mouth gaping. Sophie felt herself slip back. One hand flashed out and grasped the disc. The snake began to thrash from side to side. Sophie hung on with her other hand too. She could feel the creature's roars of anger rumbling

93

beneath her.

"I'm sorry," she cried. "I'm normally dead against cruelty to animals."

She gave a sudden hard tug. The disc mushed in her hands and broke off with an easy splop. She'd been expecting a life or death struggle, so the force she'd used sent her tumbling back into the mud.

The snake shuddered to a halt, hissing grumpily. Its coils unwound in a long, flowing movement. George and Julian slipped to the ground, gasping and coughing. The snake slowly twisted its head first one way, then the other. It slithered around the field, trying to work out where it was, and in which direction its friends had gone.

Sophie, George and Julian staggered away through the belting rain to the safety of the theatre. As they passed the sensors which surrounded it, dazzling floodlights blinked on above them, just as they had blinked on before George and Sophie gained entrance to the warship. None of the Paxi bothered to come and investigate. They'd already been caught out once that way tonight.

In the theatre's dressing-room, Sophie and George sipped delicately at mugs of tea. They'd wrapped themselves in thick blankets left over from a production of *Comets On Ice*, but they hadn't stopped shivering yet. Sophie kept having to put her tea down to wipe snake yuck off her hands.

"The Paxi grow spaceships," she mumbled, "they use trained monsters to do their dirty work, they force me to inflict harm on their trained monsters to stop them doing their dirty work... When I write this up for the school newspaper, I shall be asking for comments from the animal welfare organizations."

George wondered whether he ought to tell her that the snake would have felt no more than a pinprick, and that its disc would already have grown back. He wondered some more while he sipped his tea for twenty minutes. Oh, go on, might as well let her know.

"And that's supposed to make me feel better, is it?" said Sophie, once he had. She squeezed little clumps of damp grass out of her hair. "Ottershaw Hits Bottom: I Wrestled With Alien Menace, Claims Girl Reporter."

"I thought you were very brave, actually," said George. "You were right. Now and again, there are horrible things out there. You have to deal with them."

Sophie's eyes narrowed. Was this leading up to another of his stupid comments? Hmm, no, apparently it wasn't.

"Yes, well... Thank you," she said, trying to smooth the wrinkles in her clothes. "We wouldn't have escaped at all without you knowing what to do. So we both did pretty well." She looked down at herself. "No harm done, I suppose," she mumbled through gritted teeth. "Mud washes out. I expect snake blood does too." She pulled the wet and tatty remains of her notebook out of her pocket.

Julian bustled in. He, too, was wrapped in a blanket, but while George and Sophie were blue with cold, he was purple with fury.

"Vandals!" he croaked hoarsely. His windpipe hadn't taken kindly to being crushed by giant serpents. "Savages! Those wretched Paxi have ripped up half the seats in the auditorium! They've used every last smear of make-up to draw pictures on the stage curtains! And … and they've wee-weed into the band's instruments!"

"That's what they do, Julian," said George. "They're a vicious invading force. They're not going to put on frilly shirts and sit around discussing trends in interior decor, are they?"

Julian fiddled nervously with the broken spotlight he'd found stuffed down the loo. "It's like the first night of *Wind in the Willows* at the Saturn Hippodrome all over again."

"The point is, that climate-control unit out there is still in one piece," said George. "Destroy it, and we stand a chance of halting the invasion… I just haven't the foggiest how to, yet. It'll be surrounded by warriors and built like the back end of an Andromedan stunt elephant. We've got a head start on the

Paxi, at least. They'll be assuming the snakes have eaten us."

The thought of being eaten made Julian come over a bit queasy and he had to lie down on the floor for a moment. He dabbed at his forehead with a tissue.

"If we can't deal with the whole thing ourselves," said Sophie. "We'll have to fetch help."

George looked up at the ceiling and sighed. "Space is very, very big. The nearest planet with inhabitants daft enough to fight the Paxi is light years away. By the time we got back, the whole of Earth would be nothing but marshland dotted with really huge laser cannons. This theatre can zip along at quite a speed, but it's not THAT fast."

"Is it faster than the *Pulverizer*?" said Sophie.

George's face wriggled about a bit as he thought. "Yeh, I guess it is. We can certainly manoeuvre faster. A warship that size is pretty cumbersome."

"Well then," said Sophie. "That's our advantage. We take off slowly and let them think they can catch us. We'd at least draw them off the planet and into space for a while. Give Earth's defences a chance to move in, maybe even blow up the climate-control unit."

"Genius," grinned George. "It'll probably be left down here. You know, to make sure it stays nice and gloomy for them while they're away. They chase us round the Moon a couple of times, then we whiz back here at full speed and take cover while the big boys blast 'em. Risky but brilliant."

There was, of course, something very important he'd forgotten. Something about Paxi invasion tactics.

Julian had forgotten it, too. He dabbed his eyes with his tissue. "Such moving and heroic sentiments. The chilly wind of fear vanishes from my heart when I hear so bold and forthright an idea. It all reminds me of my days entertaining the troops in the Reticuli Galaxy. You'll forgive me if I shed a tear or two." He suddenly sat up and looked at George in alarm. "You do know how to operate the engines, don't you, dear boy?"

"Yes Julian," sighed George.

Julian smiled weakly and put away his tissue. He was about to call for backstage crew to start tidying up, then remembered that they were all still locked up in the Hospitality Area. He took his tissue out again.

"Better start pre-launch checks," said George.

"We ought to take off as quickly as we can," said Sophie. "They're bound to spot all the smoke."

George paused. "Smoke?"

"Err, yes," said Sophie. "When you landed.

There was lots of smoke."

"JULIAN!" yelled George. "You told me the spare parts you got were new!"

The sound of Julian's running feet was already fading into the distance. "They were new to US, old chap!" he called.

George grumbled angrily under his breath for a little while. Then he and Sophie went to the theatre's engine room.

Sophie was enormously impressed. There were display screens scrolling through miles of numbers. There were dials and switches and the occasional flashing light. There were strange metallic shapes across the low ceiling and down one wall. This was what she expected from a spaceship. This would get a paragraph all to itself in her report.

"Got it all on special offer," said George proudly. "Fifty per cent discount at Starships 'R' Us Hardware Warehouse, AND I got them to chuck in a free roll of carpet for the foyer. The whole propulsion system runs on a magnetic resonance wave interface, you see. That's why it shouldn't smoke."

Sophie nodded wisely, as if she knew exactly how a magnetic resonance wave interface worked. A control module next to her pinged and announced in a tiny voice that the proton unit was full. Sophie raised her eyebrows and pointed to it, as if she knew how a proton unit worked.

"We don't even need to steer or anything," continued George. "It's all automatic. You set the co-ordinates of where you're going, then you unhook the primary power distributors, then set the matter/anti-matter field, then off you go."

"Ahh," said Sophie, as if she knew how any of it worked.

Of course, George didn't know how most of it worked, either. The instruction book had been lost long ago, and fitting spare parts always took him days. He just knew what things were called and which buttons to press. Right now, the button he needed to press was the one marked "Commence Launch Sequence".

Click.

The theatre gave a gentle shudder, like a giant waking up in a cold cave. A low hum of power shook the wet grass around it. Any ants who hadn't already been drowned by the torrential rain decided enough was enough and formed a long line ready to set off in search of a new home.

Smoke began to rise from around the base of the theatre. Inside, George noticed the smoke and showed off his extensive collection of alien swearwords.

The brick-effect walls began to creak as the theatre lifted a few millimetres. It left behind a deep, roughly square dent in the ground. The hum began to rise in pitch and get steadily louder. The sound drifted out across the fields.

"Can you hear something?" said Sophie's mum, wishing her mobile phone still worked. The rest of the Earthlings in the Hospitality Area thought they could hear something too.

"E flat minor," mumbled Sophie's dad, wishing he had his piano.

Everyone was huddled into one corner of the Area. They were enjoying a makeshift show which the theatre staff were putting on to help keep their spirits up. The Great Projecto stepped into the light of a pocket torch that belonged to one of the band.

"Ladies and gentlemen," he announced. "Last ... and definitely least ... an act which has been banned in twelve star systems ... for being rubbish. As you know, ladies and gentlemen, we've had to make do with whatever props we could lay our hands on, so please bear with us. Because now! We present! Dennis Biggs and his Tent of Terror!"

Everyone clapped politely. The torch was shone on Dennis, who bowed. He held up his hands for silence, but he had it already.

"Good evening," he said in his special doom-laden voice. "Despite constant interference from one of my so-called fellow performers, I have for you tonight a trick of complete splendidness! You'll be amazed! You'll be gobsmacked! You won't boo, whatever a certain person might think!"

The hum had risen to a whirling, whooshing sound. Behind Dennis, the theatre moved into view. It glided above the top of the fence surrounding the Hospitality Area. Slowly, it rose into the night sky, trailing smoke behind it.

Dennis hadn't noticed it, and he hadn't noticed that the audience weren't looking at him any more. They burst into wild applause. He grinned an oh-thank-you-thank-you grin. Then he aimed a hand gesture at the Great Projecto that was disgustingly rude in three galactic sectors and a bit rude in another six.

"Now that IS a brilliant trick," said the headmaster, gazing into the sky.

"I expect it's done very cleverly with wires," said Mrs Womsey.

"They're not going without us, are they?" said the Great Projecto.

"I hope they don't think we're going without them," said George. He switched on a screen above his head, and he and Sophie could see the fields getting steadily smaller beneath them.

"Look at that fenced-off area!" cried Sophie. "All those people! They've got the whole town in there!" That gave her another idea: "Our Night Of Hell: Pupils Speak Out

On Being Trapped With Headmaster!" She reached into her pocket, forgetting that her notebook had turned into muddy mush. There was a squelchy noise.

George was concentrating on the warship *Pulverizer*. It was a dark blob on the screen, encircled by fields, trees, roads.

"Come on, Paxi," he said quietly. "Chase us. You're watching us, I know you are. Come on."

The warship stayed put.

"Any minute now," said George. "Any minute now... They'll chase us..."

The warship stayed put.

"They'll take ooooff... Now! Any minute now..."

"They're not coming, are they?" said Sophie.

"No."

"Surely they're not going to let us escape? Aren't they going to try to stop us?"

Suddenly George felt as if his stomach was trying to crawl out through his belly button. He'd remembered something. Something about Paxi invasion tactics. Something he should have remembered sooner.

"You ... utter ... prat," he moaned to himself, pressing his hands to his face.

"Huh?" said Sophie, nervously.

The stinger pods planted around the edge of the town had finished quietly digesting missiles. They had waited, with their long stings

103

wound tightly beneath their petals. Now they had something new to knock out of the sky.

CHAPTER EIGHT

ZZZZZZ-WHHWHHHAKKKKKK!

Buzzing blue-white sheets of electrical energy exploded through the engine room. George and Sophie were knocked off their feet. With their hair smoking slightly, they watched one screen after another fizz and go dark. The flashing lights surged with power, fluttered for a few moments, then gave up on a bad job and blinked out.

The high, whooshing hum that had been all around them began to subside. It seemed to slump, like treacle slurping down a plughole, until it turned into an endless, low groaning sound. The whole theatre shuddered.

"Am I going dizzy or has the floor tilted?" said Sophie.

George wasn't sure either. He shook his head violently. Then he put out a hand to steady himself until the sicky feeling caused by shaking his head violently went away. "It's the floor," he said. "They've blown the guidance systems. We're not dropping out of the sky, so we must have just enough power left to keep us in flight."

"Let's go and see what's happening," said Sophie.

George found he couldn't nod without feeling woozy, so he simply went, "Mmm."

They staggered out of the engine room and wobbled their way up two flights of stairs to the backstage area. They staggered and wobbled because the building was at an angle of about thirty degrees.

Julian was untangling himself from the ropes which operated the stage curtains. As soon as he unwound the last one, gravity sent him tumbling into the lighting controls. "My theatre!" he mumbled. "My beautiful theatre! All those fabulous shows, all those wonderful performers, all the happy smiling faces out there in the audience! And it's come to this. Smashed up and slightly sideways."

"Less of that, Julian," said George. "We're not beaten yet!"

He unhooked the catches on the tall sash window next to the control console and flung it open. Cold, wet air slapped around his face. Sophie held on to him while he leaned out to see around the corner of the theatre and get a look at the ground. He pulled himself back in and wiped the rain off his face with his sleeve.

"We're a few thousand feet up," he said.

A wisp of cloud moved vertically up past the window.

"And we're falling," he added. "Slowly."

"Oh great," said Sophie. She sat on a pile of costumes to stop the others seeing that her legs were shaking.

"Of course! That's why we're at an angle," said George, thinking aloud. "The engines are the heaviest things. So we're going engines first. The power left in them is slowing our descent. But as the power gets used up…"

"We'll fall faster and faster," said Sophie.

"My theatre!" mumbled Julian. "My beautiful theatre! All those fabulous shows, all those wonderful—"

A sudden volley of creaks and cracks could be heard in the distance. Gravity, age and failing engines were starting to take their toll on the Galactic Coliseum. The three of them tried to think of something else, very quickly. George came up with an idea which ditched their feelings of doom and filled them all with hope instead.

"We can use the escape capsule that's bolted to the outside wall! There, Julian, aren't you glad I had one fitted? Makes paying those few credits for it worthwhile, doesn't it?"

Then Sophie came up with an idea which emptied out their hope and put their feelings of doom right back where they'd been before.

"Hang on. Where are we falling TO, exactly? What are we going to fall ON?"

George shrugged. "The guidance systems are out. How can we tell?"

"Surely we can calculate our direction somehow?"

George pointed to the control console. "The computers in there could probably work it out, if I spoke nicely to them. But there's no point. The whole town is deserted. It doesn't matter where we crash."

"It might do," said Sophie. She gave him a you-know-what-I'm-thinking-don't-you look.

"Look, I know what you're thinking," said George. "The chances of smashing into all those people down there are tiny. It's one place in a whole area full of places. We cannot, CANNOT be that unlucky."

He spoke nicely to the computers.

"OK, we CAN be that unlucky," he said three minutes later. Julian went to fetch a mop and bucket from the cleaning cupboard. He'd decided, as captain of the ship, that if the ship was going down, it would jolly well go down with as many floors tidied as he could manage in ... how long?

"About twenty minutes, at a guess," said George.

"We can't get more power into the engines, right?" said Sophie, screwing up her eyes in concentration.

"Right," said George.

"And by the time the people below see we're heading for them, they'll be strawberry jam."

"Jam," said George.

"We can't slow down and we can't warn them," said Sophie. "Soooo..."

They looked at each other blankly. George snapped his fingers. "Maybe we can blast the theatre apart in mid-air!"

Julian let out a squeal.

"No," said George. "All the rubble would just drop on them even more quickly."

Julian let out a sigh of relief.

"Then we have to change course," said Sophie.

"With almost no power, and with no guidance system," said George.

"I'll be polishing the brasswork in the foyer if anyone needs me," trembled Julian. He picked up his mop and headed up the sloping stage.

"That foyer is a big empty space," said Sophie, mostly to herself. She was trying to remember the piece she'd written about Ms Sternback, the school's Head of Science, and her theories on an object's centre of gravity.

"Yeeeh..." said George, not sure what she was on about. "It IS a big empty space. You've got to get the audience in and out somehow."

"Listen! The engines are doing their best to

hold us up in the air," said Sophie. "They're balancing the whole building or we'd be tumbling over and over. Simple physics, yes?"

"Yeeeh..." said George, still not sure what she was on about.

"So what if the weight inside the building shifted? I mean, enough to affect the balance?"

"The engines are programmed to compensate, of course," said George, grinning. "If they try to regain balance, they'll have to move to one side, and if they move to one side..."

"We change course," said Sophie.

"It'll mean losing the last of the power. We'll drop like a stone. Or rather, we'll drop like a whacking great theatre."

"That escape capsule of yours had better work."

George ran up the stage and jumped into the orchestra pit. "Come on then! Let's stop yattering and get it done! The higher up we are, the smaller the shift we need to miss those people! MOVE!"

The Paxi had ripped up half the seats in the auditorium in order to be nasty and to cause as many credits' worth of damage as possible. If they'd known that all those broken chairs were destined to become a useful tool in the battle against them, they'd never have bothered.

"They could have smashed them into smaller pieces, though," grunted George, hauling two heavy lumps of row C out into the foyer.

Julian was delighted. "Splendid! Many hands make light work, when it comes to cleaning-up operations."

"Julian, get everything into this foyer NOW! Seats, curtains, costumes, everything! We need weight on the front of the building! Come ON!"

They lifted, pulled, tore and flung for all they were worth. George shifted six rows of seats, fourteen stage lights and whatever pieces of scenery he could find. Sophie shifted five and a half rows of seats, two dozen assorted boxes of props from backstage and most of the contents of the dressing-room. Julian shifted an empty make-up bag.

"Hey, I've just thought," gasped George, struggling with a trunk full of shoes.

"What?" wheezed Sophie, heaving an armful of costumes.

"If we do manage to shift the theatre over a bit, we might land right on the *Pulverizer*."

"Now hear this, or else! All decks at battle alert!" The voice of the guard on emergency shouting duty echoed through the Paxi warship. "All crew report to panic stations! Theatrical building moving on to collision course! And if, umm, if you're doing us the honour of listening to this announcement, Commander

… we, err, humbly await your noble and completely glorious orders, sir."

"Creep," muttered Commander Ix in his cabin. He hated being woken up, and he REALLY hated being woken up from lovely dreams about death and destruction. He pressed the button beside his bed marked "Cancel Emergency Shouting". Once the guard's yelps of pain had died away, he pressed the button marked "Instruction Channel". A tiny screen flipped up from his pillow, and Ko's face appeared.

"Get my shuttle pod ready for launch," gurgled Commander Ix. "And bring warriors. I've had enough of being nice to these Earthlings."

"Instantly, Commander!"

Ix pressed the button marked "To the Shuttle Pod!" The bed beneath him slurped aside and he dropped into a wide tube coated with grease. Seconds later he plopped out of the other end of the tube, on to the flight deck of the shuttle. Ko, at the steering wheel in front of him, stood and saluted.

"Let's go," said Commander Ix.

The fat, bulbous shuttle lifted off from the main body of the ship like a piece breaking off from the side of a cake. It twisted around in mid-air to face the theatre, then shot upwards.

"Wait! I can feel movement. It's regaining balance," said George.

Sophie could feel movement too. She could also feel a fluttering in her stomach.

"We're starting to fall faster," said George. "The power could give out at any second. Then we'll drop."

"Let's get to the escape capsule," said Sophie.

"My thoughts precisely, dear girl," trembled Julian, nervously tugging at the ends of his moustache. "Our work here is done. We can rest easy in our beds, secure in the knowledge that we have saved the day. Now let's leg it."

They legged it as far as the auditorium, but a sudden explosion of metal and plastic which shot across the orchestra pit stopped them in their tracks. They turned to see that a jagged hole had been blasted in the side of the building. Wind and rain poured in. Through the hole they could see Ix's shuttle pod. It had matched the theatre's course and speed and was now flying parallel to it.

The shuttle's airlock, facing the jagged hole in the wall, hissed open. One after another, two dozen Paxi warriors jumped the gap between shuttle and theatre and scuttled across the auditorium. Ko and Commander Ix were the last ones out. Ko was bent forwards with the weight of a toolbox strapped to his shoulders. Ix squashed his helmet tightly on to his head and pointed at the three humans.

"Get them."

They legged it again. They hadn't gone two metres before two dozen warriors piled on top of them, cackling and slobbering.

"ONE of you get them!" bellowed Ix. "The rest of you fix the engines! Stop this thing falling on to my lovely warship!"

Ko led all but one of the warriors away. The remaining one dived at the three humans. They quickly rolled out of the way, jumped to their feet and scattered.

"Which of the human scumbags shall I get first, Commander?" said the warrior.

Ix's dripping tongue licked across his lips. "Doesn't matter, soldier. They can't get away. We'll catch them one by one. And one by one they'll suffer the vengeance of Ix of the Hydrax League."

"Now now," burbled Julian. "Surely we can all sit down and discuss our differences in a civilized manner? Perhaps with a cup of tea and a nice crumbly biscuit?"

Ix lurched at him, mouth wide open. Julian scampered behind Sophie.

"Or perhaps not," said Julian.

"Julian, Sophie," said George, not taking his eyes off the two Paxi. "Let's move slowly towards ... where we were going. Mr Ix here is right. We, err, can't escape, can we? No harm in us, umm, walking around a bit, is there?"

114

He stepped back, in the direction of a door on the opposite side of the auditorium. Above the door glowed a bright green EXIT sign.

The warrior shuffled around behind him, blocking his path. George stood still. He stared at Ix. Ix stared at him.

"You've got an escape capsule out there, haven't you?" said Ix with a smile. "Nice try."

He unhooked the weapon from the chest plate of his armour and gave it a hard squeeze. A twisting purple bolt of energy leapt at the beautifully decorated ceiling. Huge slabs of it split off and crashed to the ground, blocking the exit. They also knocked the Paxi warrior senseless. Ix hurried over to him and gave him a kick.

"How dare you, soldier! Unconscious on duty without permission! You are below standard!" With a second squeeze, Ix zapped him into a smear of green goo.

George took advantage of Ix's back being turned. "Out the window!" he cried.

The three of them bounded for the stage. The window by the control console was still wide open, as George had left it. Ix bounded too, and caught Julian in a perfect rugby tackle. Once he'd stopped screaming, Julian managed to splutter: "I'll hold him off! Get to the capsule and meet me by the main entrance!"

George and Sophie hesitated for a moment,

then turned and headed for the window. Holding on to the wooden frame, George jumped straight out on to the window ledge. Sophie stuck her head out. Damp, icy wind stung her cheeks and eyes.

To one side of the window, clamped to the wall and weaving their way down the building, were a series of heating tubes which had been moulded to look like drainpipes. Beyond them, illuminated by the distant lightning, was the curved shape of the escape capsule, attached to the wall.

Sophie took a deep breath and climbed out of the window. Her hand slipped on the wet drainpipe. For a second she thought she would fall, but her reflexes pulled her muscles tight and she held on.

Behind them, on the stage, Julian and Commander Ix fought like cat and dog. Well, like slightly weedy Earthling and menacing slimy alien, anyway. Ix hurled Julian to the floor. Julian's arm landed within reach of a broken stage light. He grabbed it and swung it with every atom of strength he had. He had very few atoms of strength, so the light bounced uselessly off the side of Ix's head. The commander reached down and dragged Julian off the floor by his ears.

"I'll save your torture until my warriors can return to enjoy it with me," he whispered. "They'll be back in a minute. The engines will soon be fixed."

But down in the engine room:

"Engines badly damaged, sir. Fixing may not be possible," reported the warrior in charge of repairs. He saluted Ko and continued with his work.

Ko was getting nervous. He tried to decide which was worse: being killed by Commander Ix for failing to carry out orders or being killed by a few thousand tonnes of falling theatre. He couldn't decide, so instead he tried to work out a plan for getting back to Ix's shuttle and saving his own skin, but the busy scuttling of warriors around the engine room kept distracting him.

"Power at one per cent of normal and falling," reported the warrior in charge of bad news. "Prepare for sudden drop! Power failure in thirty seconds ... twenty-nine seconds ... twenty-eight seconds..."

The theatre groaned. The engines wound down to a mousey squeak.

"Twenty-seven seconds ... twenty-six seconds..."

CHAPTER NINE

Freezing air cut into Sophie's fingers. She couldn't feel the drainpipe she was clinging on to. George was one pipe further along, and slightly below her. Raindrops trickled down her face.

Twenty-five seconds ... twenty-four seconds...

"I c-can't ... I'm f-frozen..." she cried.

"You can, you can!" called George. "The power could go any time now!" The capsule was only a couple of metres away.

He shifted from one pipe to the next. The metal bracket holding the pipe to the wall bent and snapped. The pipe swung loose. George scrambled madly. His feet bicycled in mid-air. The movement snapped a second bracket, higher up. The pipe began to give way.

Eighteen seconds...

Sophie reached down, but George was too

far away to grab on to. He leapt to one side. The pipe broke away beneath him and spun out of sight. His hand locked on to the metal frame which held the escape capsule attached to the wall.

Fifteen seconds...

Two grappling figures appeared at the window they had come through. Commander Ix kept swatting Julian aside. Julian kept walloping Commander Ix with the arm of row B, seat 12. Ix took aim. Sophie shut her eyes.

Zzzzzzz-AAPPPPP!

The escape capsule shattered into tiny strips. It blew away on the wind like a cloud sucked into a tornado. George was left dangling from what remained of its metal frame.

Howling with laughter, Ix waddled back to the stage, dragging Julian behind him. Sophie and George looked around, as if expecting something to come along and save them at the last minute. It didn't.

"Oh crumbs," said George.

"What more can happen to us?" wailed Sophie.

Two seconds ... one second...

"Listen!" cried George. "No engines!"

"OH NOO$_{\text{O}_{\text{O}_{\text{O}_{\text{O}_{\text{O}_{\text{o}}}}}}}$!"

*   *   *

In the engine room, the fall sent warriors flying in all directions. Being Paxi, it'd take more than a sudden drop to make them be sick all over the place. On the other hand, being Paxi, they were sick all over the place anyway.

The warrior in charge of repairs managed to hold on to the toolkit and stay put. Ko ordered him to ignore the stuff splashing over the back of his head and keep working.

Up on stage, Commander Ix was having fun. He was getting a weird, weightless feeling, which made it easier for him to twirl Julian round and round by his hair. Julian found that the only sound he could make was, "WwooOOooowwooOOoowwooOO."

Outside, Ix's shuttle pod was dropping out of the sky too. Its programming told it to fly alongside the theatre, next to the hole in the wall of the auditorium. But its thrusters and its on-board computer couldn't keep up. It started to spin and weave. It tumbled back along the wall, trying to steady itself.

On the other side of the building, Sophie couldn't hold on much longer. The cold had numbed her arm completely. All she could see was George fluttering from the remains of the escape capsule's frame like a handkerchief on a washing line. All she could hear was the howling wind. All she could think of was the ground hurtling up to meet them and the sickening smash that would engulf them at any second.

Nothing could stop it now.

"Sir!" cried the warrior in charge of repairs. Ko had his arms wrapped around his head. He was trying desperately to remember if he'd been mean enough to his relatives in his will.

"SIR!" yelled the warrior. Ko tightened his arms. How could he concentrate with this INFERNAL RACKET going on?

"SIIIRRRRRR!"

"WHAT?"

"Power line resealed! Do I have permission to restart engines, sir?"

"Yesyesyesyesyes!" screamed Ko.

The warrior flipped the engines to maximum. A massive surge of power ...

... shook the building. It slowed rapidly. The engines whined and moaned. George and Sophie, slowing much less rapidly, smacked painfully against the wall. They held on to whatever drainpipes were within reach.

"They've done it!" cried Sophie. "They've stopped us crashing!"

"Yeh," said George. "They've also well and truly beaten us now."

Suddenly Ix's shuttle, still swerving and

trying to tell left from right, flew up around the corner of the building and loomed over their heads. It jumped towards them.

Sophie gasped and curled up into a knot. George aimed a kick at one of its control panels as it dipped low. Its airlock opened with a sharp hiss.

"Sophie," he said with a grin, "forget what I said about being beaten. Get in."

In the auditorium, the sudden slowing-down jolt had brought Julian joy and misery. Joy: he was hurled free and landed on the floor next to the hole in the wall. Misery: Ix landed on top of him.

The commander grunted happily and rolled to his feet. He gurgled and clapped. The engines were fixed, exactly as he'd ordered. He would see to it personally that the warrior in charge of repairs received the most generous reward any of his troops had ever been given. Not one, but TWO entire minutes on easy duties. Now it was time to reboard his shuttle. He stepped out through the hole in the wall.

The shuttle was gone.

Ix made a deep dent in the roof of the warship fifty metres below and lay there blinking. Where had it...?

The shuttle zigzagged overhead. Inside, George was in Ko's driving seat, stabbing madly at buttons.

"You mean you can't actually FLY this thing?" wailed Sophie.

"I've never had the chance before, have I?" cried George.

Sophie sank into Ix's chair and held on tight. There was no time to worry about the slime that was sticking to the back of her legs. The shuttle lurched up, right, left, down, up again.

Commander Ix's voice suddenly crackled from speakers all around them. "If humans are on my shuttle, GET OUT! I order you to submit to the might of the Paxi! I order you to surrender and be liquidated immediately! HUUUMANS!"

George switched the speakers off and adjusted the flight controls. "I think I'm getting the hang of it now," he said calmly. The shuttle banked steeply, then flew level. On a screen in front of them the Paxi climate-control unit swung into view.

George looked at Sophie. Sophie looked at George.

"So, do you reckon this shuttle could survive the impact?" she said.

"Yeh," said George. "Just about."

Sophie covered her eyes.

George yanked a lever at his side. The shuttle's thrusters roared and it suddenly shot forward at full speed. With a thundering crash, it whopped into the front of the climate-control unit. With a crashing thunder, it whopped out through the other side.

The unit's inner workings burst apart in a stream of swirling light. It spluttered and dimmed. Its sides sank and it gradually collapsed in on itself. At last it shrivelled into a grey and slightly steaming heap.

The shuttle, now battered and smoking, shuddered to the ground. It landed with a thump in the field behind the *Pulverizer*, gouging a long furrow in the earth before sliding to a halt.

Meanwhile, the theatre slowed to a dead stop two and a half millimetres from Commander Ix's bulging eyes. It hovered steadily, its loud hum making the air throb. Then, piloted by the repair team in the engine room, it slowly moved away. It tilted upright and came in to land a short distance from where it had originally stood.

George and Sophie shoved at the shuttle's airlock and it dropped off its hinges. They stepped out on to the grass, water squelching around their shoes. They both wobbled slightly.

"You OK?" George said at last.

"I think so," said Sophie weakly. "Have I suffered a blow to the head or is it getting lighter?"

It had stopped raining too. They trudged around to the front of the theatre. Ko and the repair team were scuttling away to their ship, heads down to avoid the warmth. There was a gap in the clouds above them, through which shone rays of bright, early morning sunlight. As George and Sophie watched, the gap got wider and wider until the last of the clouds evaporated. The sky was a clean, clear blue.

"Wow," said Sophie, blinking.

"Weather control units are tough bits of machinery," said George. "Takes a bit of a whack to put a hole in one. But when they go, they really go, don't they?"

The area around the warship was a tangle of Paxi warriors shouting commands, getting confused and fighting over the last patches of shade. Ix, fumbling for a pair of sunglasses, crawled out of his dent in the warship's roof and scurried for cover.

He gave orders for a brand-new, radically different plan to be put into effect. This involved leaving Earth as fast as possible. He ordered that this new plan be called "fearless and forward-thinking". He also ordered that anyone using the word "retreat" would be shoved in the fry-up at suppertime. Then he ordered that the name *Pulverizer* on the side of the ship be painted out and replaced with *My Whole Planet's Gonna Get You, Earthling WORMS, So WATCH IT!*

Paxi patrols, who had been out and about breaking things all night, appeared one by one. They ran for the damp darkness of the ship, cowering beneath torn-off car doors and ripped-up carpets.

A high-pitched warbling noise suddenly blasted out from the ship. George clapped his hands over his ears.

"Homing signal!" he shouted. "Activates brain-control chips implanted in their bio-weapons!" Sophie didn't hear him, because she had her hands clapped over her ears too.

The swamp snakes appeared within minutes. They were lazy beasts at heart and hadn't gone far. A wide hatch dropped open on the underside of the ship and they slithered out of sight. The Twinkles took longer to turn up. Unlike the snakes, they had roamed for miles. Once the last one was aboard, the signal fluttered away to silence. Meanwhile, the stinger pods that surrounded the town began to wither and die in the heat of the morning sun.

George and Sophie watched as the warship gave a whirr of power and rose higher and higher into the sky. Finally, it changed course sharply and vanished from sight at high speed.

"Victory!" cried Julian. He marched out of the theatre's main entrance, arms wide and grin even wider. "Truth, justice and law and order have triumphed over that rotten rabble! A single tear rolls down my cheek, my dear friends, in honour of our valiant battle, of our wonderful team spirit, and the hundreds of credits it'll cost to get those seats fixed."

George and Sophie paid no attention to him.

"We're safe now, right?" said Sophie.

George shrugged. "I don't think the Paxi have ever been defeated before. They'll be really embarrassed. Too embarrassed to come back, anyway. Looks like we did a good job."

"Yes," smiled Sophie. "We did." She looked over at the tall fences that enclosed the Hospitality Area. "Come on. Better start getting things back to normal."

It took George forty-seven minutes and fifty-two seconds to decode the electronic locks on the Hospitality Area gates and open them up. It took one minute, fifteen seconds for everyone in the Hospitality Area to stampede to freedom.

Dennis Biggs, the Great Projecto, Douglas the android (and his cardboard box), the headmaster, Mrs Womsey, the rest of the school, the residents of Paradise Street and Murray Road. They all came thundering out in one huge multi-legged mass. They broke up and scattered across the fields, heading to whatever was left of their homes.

"Mum!" cried Sophie.

Sophie's mum dashed right past her. She straightened her crumpled suit with one hand and tapped numbers into her mobile phone with the other. Now that the Paxi jamming signals had gone, she could get back to business. "Yeh! Hi!" she barked into the phone.

127

"Slight delay. Alien invasion or something. Call a meeting of the board. Full presentation of the new sales attack plan over lunch!"

"Mum!"

She hurried away, brushing mud off her briefcase. Dad wandered past.

"Dad!"

Sophie's voice disturbed the train of musical notes running through his head. He stopped suddenly and raised a finger. Without looking up, he hummed the exact note on which Sophie had spoken.

"Mmmmmm... D sharp? Oh dear, no no no no no!"

He tramped across the fields. He would find the nearest piano and continue composing his new symphony without the aid of D sharp. Sophie watched him disappear behind an overturned bus on the road behind the theatre.

From the theatre itself came the sounds of a party starting up. The band were gathering together their rusty instruments and the backstage crew were building makeshift tables to hold a celebration feast. The broken food dispensers turned out nothing except mashed-up cucumber sandwiches, but they made the best of things. Only a few of the sandwiches were thrown at Julian. George kept wondering where Sophie had got to.

Sophie was back at home. She was thinking carefully about something very important.

CHAPTER TEN

Extract from the next day's *Local Evening Telegraph*:

TOWN FURY
OVER HOOLIGANS

The town council held an emergency public meeting last night. On the agenda was the outrage felt by the community at the severe vandalism suffered by the town and the recent imprisonment of residents by alien nasties from beyond the stars.

Several alarmed citizens called for a ban on spaceship parking in the town centre. Prominent local teacher Mrs Eileen Womsey urged those present to begin a project studying alien culture, in the interests of interplanetary peace and harmony. A more sensible approach was adopted by the headmaster at the centre of the recent Monster Attacks School incident. He pointed out that there was no evidence to suggest aliens had been involved. "The whole thing was obviously a publicity gimmick, set up by the town's cinema to advertize some new science-fiction nonsense," he commented. "I shall be writing to the Government to complain in the strongest possible terms about such irresponsible, ill-mannered behaviour. And I could tell that spaceship was made of cardboard, too!"

With a deep sigh, Sophie folded up the newspaper and dropped it into the kitchen swingbin. "Twits," she mumbled. "A dead bee's got more sting than that report."

She gave her readers at the school a detailed account of the invasion, of the *Pulverizer*, and of how Earth had escaped a hideous fate. Nobody believed a word of it. She did an interview with Julian, in which he spoke at great length about his time as a stand-up comic at the Constellation Club on Mars. Nobody believed a word of that either. She also did an interview with Douglas the android, but all she could get out of him was a smile and a little robot mouse he'd made from an old DVD player. She didn't bother publishing that one.

It took many hours' work to get the theatre back to normal. George was kept extremely busy organizing replacement seats, mending machinery and stopping Dennis and the Great

Projecto from clobbering each other. But at last posters appeared all over town announcing a grand farewell performance "in aid of the Galactic Coliseum Restoration Fund", to be followed by lift-off at precisely 10p.m.

"Ladies and gentlemen!" announced Julian. "The final act in tonight's show is TOTALLY unsuitable for children!"

The audience went, "Urrrrrr."

The auditorium was packed. The band played spooky noises as the terrifying spectacle of Dennis Biggs and his Wardrobe of Mystery was played out before them. At its nerve-tingling climax, Dennis's volunteer from the audience, Mrs Womsey, stepped out of the wardrobe to be greeted with wild applause. Her face and hair had been transformed into a dazzling explosion of bright colours. She returned to her seat smiling blankly. She couldn't see herself, so she had no idea what the fuss was about.

Dennis bowed and blew kisses to the audience as the curtain descended in front of him. Julian appeared at the side of the stage, walking with a dramatic limp he'd been practising for ages.

"Ladies and gentlemen! Bravely the forces of good, including me, have sent the forces of darkness packing. But worry not about my ... terrible sufferings. The pills will keep the pain at bay. Let us say our goodbyes, ladies and gentlemen, after which may I ask you to kindly stand well back in the field outside, as we will be firing up the anti-gravity drive. Our show is at an end and we must be on our way to our next booking, in the Arkon Nebula. Tickets still available for all performances, by the way, micro-organisms half price. Thank you."

Sophie picked up the heavy bag she'd hidden under her front-row seat. While the band struck up a brisk showbiz tune and the performers assembled on stage for their curtain calls, she took the opportunity to sneak backstage without being noticed. George was operating the lights.

"Hi!" he said with a smile. "Come to say toodle-oo?"

"Not exactly," said Sophie. "Do you think I could call Douglas off stage for a couple of minutes? I'd like him to do his robot folding act one more time."

The audience filed out of the theatre. Sophie appeared from behind the stage curtain and caught up with the multi-coloured Mrs Womsey. At least, it looked like Sophie. She seemed to be walking in a rather mechanical way and her happy smile seemed ever so slightly crooked.

"Ah, there you are, Sophie," said Mrs Womsey. "Wasn't it a marvellous show? But there was one thing I didn't understand. Mr Biggs whispered to me that it would all wash out except the green. I've no idea what he meant, have you?"

"I have done my homework," said the Sophie robot in a squeaky voice. "I love my mummy and daddy."

"Perfect," said the real Sophie, peeking out from under the curtain. "They'll never know the difference." She had a quick check through her bag to make sure she'd brought all her favourite books with her.

"But why do you want to come with us?" said George.

"What?" said Sophie. "I can't stay here, can I? I'd miss out on the chance to see the universe!"

She watched the robot and Mrs Womsey merge into the bustle of people shuffling out through the foyer. One by one, George switched off the lights in the auditorium.

The audience stood out in the field, watching excitedly as the great Victorian bulk of the Galactic Coliseum slowly lifted off the ground. The hum of its engines rose steadily and healthily but, despite George's best efforts, a gush of smoke still billowed around its base.

The theatre glided vertically upwards, into the last blue-red streaks of the summer sunset. Stars were starting to glimmer, and soon the theatre seemed no bigger than one of them.

The audience all agreed that this was still the best trick they'd ever seen.

The theatre continued on its way. From that night onwards, Sophie transmitted regular bulletins back to Earth newspapers. She caused quite a stir with her first report: "The Moon Is Hollow – Ottershaw Has Proof".